PULP LITERATURE PRESS

Issue No. 35, Summer 2022

Publisher: Pulp Literature Press; Managing Editor: Jennifer Landels; Senior Editor: Mel Anastasiou; Acquisitions Editor: Genevieve Wynand; Poetry Editors: Daniel Cowper & Emily Osborne; Assistant Editors: Brooklynn Hook, Nik Kos, Melisa Gruger; Copy Editor: Amanda Bidnall; Proofreader: Mary Rykov; Graphic Design: Amanda Bidnall; Cover Design: Kate Landels; First Readers: Samantha Olson, Carol McCauley, Brenda Carre, Jeya Thiessen; Subscriptions: Carol McCauley; Advertising: Brooklynn Hook. For advertising rates, direct inquiries to info@pulpliterature.com.

Cover painting, *Collector* by Akem. Artwork for 'The Play's the Thing' by Allison Bannister and Tom O'Brien. All other illustrations by Mel Anastasiou.

Pulp Literature: ISSN 2292-2164 (Print), ISSN 2292-2172 (Digital), Issue No. 35, Summer 2022.

Pulp Literature Press gratefully acknowledges the support of the Canada Council for the Arts.

Canada Council   Conseil des arts
for the Arts   du Canada

Pulp Literature is a proud member of the Magazine Association of BC and Magazines Canada.

TABLE OF CONTENTS

FROM THE PULP LIT PULPIT

Ordinary Magic

Have you ever danced the Macarena? Done the Running Man? Surely you've tickled Elmo or talked to the hand. Done up your 'do in a scrunchie or a flattop or the Rachel? Was it Nirvana or the Spice Girls in your Discman? And just how big was your Beanie Babies collection? Whatever your nineties style — or current retro version thereof — no trip through the decade of Docs and flannel would be complete without a solid three-minute stare at a Magic Eye poster.

Stereograms weren't new to the nineties. Binocular stereopsis — the visual sense of depth we perceive from having two eyes spaced apart — was discovered in the nineteenth century. The stereogram trend of *that* era was the Victorian stereoscope. And, beginning in 1939, it was the View-Master. But the colourful Magic Eye posters let us do the work ourselves, no device required. They take advantage of the slightly different image received by each eye, and from a two-dimensional image, we get a three-dimensional scene.

The trick is to soften your focus. Relax your gaze. Stay present. Reading, whether with your fingers, your ears, or your eyes, asks this of us too. Take in some sensory detail, translate it (neurologically *and* psychologically), and let the images come alive in your very own mind. Of course, sometimes the thing we expect to see isn't the thing we end up seeing. But a crack in the expected might just invite us into a whole new world.

Here at *Pulp*, we delight in bringing you a glimpse of the timeless beyond the trends. This issue is full of friends and family, magic and mermaids. Familiar themes, yes, but in the hands of our authors, brought to new and enchanting life. In storytelling, writers make something from nothing (ah, the dreaded blank page!). Of course, nothing is ever truly *nothing*. Blank space, white space, dark matter. Creative inspiration. There is a there *there*. It is the lucky reader who gets to discover it. Sometimes all you have to do is trust in the magic.

~Genevieve Wynand

It's summertime, and the water's fine ... or is it? 'Collector' by cover artist **Akem** beckons us beneath the surface and between the pages. But in 'A Collection of Secrets' by feature author **Rhea Rose** and 'The Island' by **M Denise Beaton**, we discover that some treasures are better left hidden.

Back on shore, summer brings around friends both new and old in 'Audrey and the Crow' by **Cadence Mandybura**, 'The Two Oh Four Six' by **Dustin Moon**, 'Floaters' by **Kevin Sandefur**, and 'Whispers in Between My Shoulder Blades' by **Christine Breede**.

Shapeshifers in 'Shadow Work' by **Soramimi Hanarejima** and 'Gwannyn's Song' by **JM Landels** show us the secret to sacrifice. And families come together, reshaped, in **Kaile Shilling**'s SiWC honourable mention, 'Death and Laughter'.

Allison Bannister in 'The Play's the Thing' and **Mel Anastasiou** in 'Pretty Lies: Hold On' draw inspiration from the classics. And poetry from **Dawn Macdonald** and **Yuan Changming** reminds us that love is classic too.

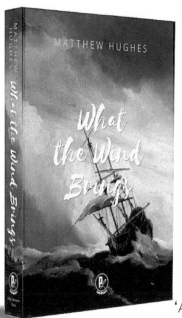

Out of the fires of a Caribbean slave revolt, shipwrecked on the jungle coast of 16th-century Ecuador, an educated slave, a shaman, and a monk hunted by the Inquisition fight for freedom against the might of Imperial Spain.

Dive into an epic slipstream novel of intrigue and adventure from fantasy author Matthew Hughes, the writer George R.R. Martin calls 'criminally underrated,' and Robert J. Sawyer says is 'a towering talent.'

'A triumph!' - Cecelia Holland
'Sensational' - Candas Jane Dorsey

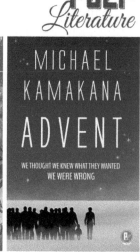

A COLLECTION OF SECRETS

Rhea Rose

Rhea Rose has published many Canadian speculative short-fiction stories and poems. She is a three-time Aurora Award nominee and is currently nominated a fourth time for her editorial work and writing in Polar Starlight, *an online zine of speculative poetry by Canadian authors. Her story 'The Gamogue' appears in* Pulp Literature *Issue 12, Autumn 2016.*

$\mathcal{A}$ Collection of Secrets

When I turned twelve, in 1967, I ordered sea monkeys from a comic book. I kept the critters in an old green Jell-O mould I'd found stuffed with cleaning rags under the kitchen sink. I'd filled it with rusty-coloured tap water, water the city warned us not to drink before boiling.

The creatures soon grew from thimble-sized to the length of my thumb—too many, too fast. By the time I moved the mould from the kitchen to my room, they'd chewed a tiny hole through the thin plastic and it had begun to leak.

I moved them quickly to a glass bowl on the dresser in the room I shared with my little sister, Taryn. Over time, the sea monkeys, each a different colour of the rainbow, escaped. But they didn't get far.

A few leapt free and landed smack on top of the dresser, where their long purple locks caught in my hairbrush and they dried out. Some dangled like golden strings of unravelled yarn, twisting around a dresser-drawer handle. Others lay draped and dehydrated, orange and limp like carrot peels, over a tube of lipstick.

An old aquarium with no fish, but all set up with plenty of aquatic plants, rocks, a bubbling treasure chest—all of it costing a total of twenty-five cents at a garage sale — solved the plastic-eating problem for a while.

Still, they escaped.

I'd find one or two of them hard and crispy in my old flip-flops, the toeholds chewed away. Two curled up behind my sunglasses, but, before they dried up, had bit perfectly round baby-finger-sized holes through the middle of each lens. Some chewed a hole through my tube of Coppertone suntan cream and drowned in the lotion. Turns out the sea monkeys I'd ordered from my Prince Valiant comic book weren't sea monkeys at all. The dehydrated dust-sized creatures I'd sprinkled into the water had grown into tiny lemon-yellow, lime-green, raspberry-red, orangey-orange, and blueberry-blue ... mermaids.

I took my secret collection of survivors down to the basement bathroom, put them into the huge, vintage clawfoot bathtub, with its rusted white porcelain — 'the spotted cheetah', I called it. My shimmer of mermaids couldn't escape the high sloping sides of the tub, and they thrived.

Then mom decided to refinish the cheetah.

Holding one at arm's length by its tail, mom dangled the most exquisite, dripping, jewel of a mermaid. This one rivalled any treasure in a collection of lovely small things. Her skin was a glistening icy blue; her indigo hair sparkled and flowed, long and wavy. Mom crinkled her nose as if she'd discovered a bag of doggy poop in her box of tampons.

She dropped the tiny mermaid onto my palm. Blue's miniature fluke bobbed, waved hello.

"Hali, tropical fish in my tub?" She lifted the lid on the toilet. "Flush them."

"No!" I screamed. "These are pets, exotic ones. They can't be *flushed*. I'll find another place." I slipped my hand deep into the cool tub water and Blue floated away. Red surfaced, took her blue sister's hand. They dove, then disappeared as a water plant umbrellaed over them.

"How many?" mom asked, peering into the water. By the time she'd discovered my secret collection, my numbers had topped at least seventy, maybe even a hundred—they were still so little.

"All in my tub?" she asked.

"Not all," I said under my breath. "Had to take a few back upstairs to Taryn's room. Besides, they like her betta fish." I didn't bother to tell her about the overfilled sink in the garage, a place mom never goes. Mom made me promise to rid the house of every 'tropical fish', except for the bettas in Taryn's aquarium.

I promised.

With my arm around her waist, I gently ushered her away from the cheetah.

After school one day, on my way through our yard, I was startled by a loud crash of broken glass in the garage. I dropped my school books and ran toward it.

I flipped on the fluorescents and headed straight for the sink. Water sloshed out over my legs, giving my white Keds and knee socks a tsunami soaking.

The water heaved again.

Oberon! Part Maine Coon, mostly stray. An outdoor killer.

His sky-blue eyes stared up from the bloody water as they rocked on the surface. Oberon's tail sailed awkwardly, no longer attached to his body. His rib cage flashed at me like streaks of white coral in dark water.

Too terrified to put my hand in the moving water where the remains of my cat swirled, I grabbed the chain attached to the sink's plug, pulled hard, and watched the water gurgle down the drain. Oberon's blue eyes and scrapped remains lay at the bottom of the sink, amongst the thrashing finger-sized mermaids.

I collected most of the mermonsters from all my water sources, using a long-handled fishnet I bought at the pet store. I caught a bunch at a time then put them in two giant Tupperware bowls, the kind with snap-down lids. I put the bowls in a large cooler with wheels and loaded it into Taryn's red wagon. We hitched the wagon to my bike and she followed me on hers.

When we got to the shore, Taryn and I manoeuvred the cooler through the sand. I pulled at the front and she guided the back. Taryn's long black hair blew into her small face as she grunted and pushed hard. But my braids and floppy wide-brimmed hat kept my red hair back.

At the ocean's edge, we rolled our pants up to our knees and waded slowly into the warm salty sea. We pulled the lids off the bowls, careful not to spill. Taryn floated one of the bowls over to me to hold. As the big yellow bowls rocked quietly, I kept my eyes on the tips of Taryn's fingers hanging onto the bowl's rim. Then, before I could stop her, she reached in and scooped out a handful of the creatures. Taryn held them near the water's surface and squealed, delighted as they slithered from between her fingers into the ocean. "Don't touch them!" I yelled.

"This is such a good idea, Hali," Taryn said, holding her bowl steady.

"Is it?" I asked, wishing Taryn's fingers away from her grip on the rim of the container.

The soft, supple mermaid bodies fit comfortably within the curves of the bowls. All pressed together at the bottom, they formed colourful jelly-like lumps, but when a bit of ocean water splashed in over them, they raced around the bowls, creating swirls of shooting colour like paint dropped onto a spinning canvas. They swam faster, circling. They became multi-coloured rainbow rings, braiding around one another.

Taryn didn't scoop out any more mermaids, but carefully tipped the bowl, and a little more of the ocean leaked in.

"They've been living in tap water and we don't want to shock their systems. We don't want to kill them," I said.

"We don't?" Taryn asked, looking puzzled.

"No, we don't," I said, reminding her that we were releasing the mermaids so they'd have a chance to survive.

Slowly, I reached over and tipped the bowls until the water in them became one with the ocean. The mermaids slipped free like so many red, yellow, pink, and blue fruity-coloured popsicles gliding into the sea. For a short while, they swam across the surface, playing, pulling hair, leaping, and looking like bits of wet, coloured cloth woven into small water tornados so hypnotic that I forgot about Oberon, what they'd done to him.

One of them ate a lamprey-bite-sized chunk from one of the plastic bowls left afloat. Another nibbled ravenously at my water shoes and bit my leg. It felt like a bee sting. The tiny mark on my calf glared red. Soon enough, they disappeared.

I heard Taryn's childish screams as she ran for shore.

"Time to go," I yelled. "We'll let another batch go next Sunday."

And we did.

Taryn and I continued to release the tiny mermaids into the ocean every Sunday. I'd put the Oberon incident out of my mind, and said no when mom offered to get another family pet. Meanwhile, Taryn developed a skin condition believed by the doctor to be caused by close contact with 'tropical fish'.

One Sunday, mom caught us as we headed out on another excursion. She'd decided that introducing a foreign species into the sea might be a bad idea. Her save-the-seas ethic came too late though, because by then Taryn and I had released at least a hundred mermaids into the ocean.

"Enough to fill an encyclopaedia," Taryn said.

Mom became preoccupied with her Amway sales and forgot about the 'tropical fish', which made it easier for me to continue to order the so-called sea monkeys. But now, I experimented with them. I discovered that they loved my music. I played mostly Led Zeppelin and Pink Floyd. The mermaids gathered on a large rock in the lidded aquarium and listened while I did my chores.

Sometimes I'd grab the salt shaker from the kitchen and sprinkle salt into their tank. They seemed to thrive in any kind of water, be it tap or salt—or even bubble baths. The mermaids loved the bubbles and would play around with them for hours. I fed them tropical fish food, scraps from my dinner plate. They ate anything I gave them. And boy, did they grow.

When Taryn and I hit our late teens, mom finally ran off with a retired bailiff to become a vanner somewhere up north.

Taryn moved out shortly after and married her high-school sweetheart.

I stayed in the old house to continue with my studies in marine biology at college — and my secret mermaid programme at home.

By then, I understood so much more.

My newest batch of creatures had each grown to the size of a pack of spaghetti. They seemed to double in size every few months. I discovered that if separated from each other and left alone in large guaranteed-to-never-leak Rubbermaid bins in the shed, the mermaids became docile — afloat with their long hair drifting, their glittering tails occasionally flicking. They lived the languid, solitary lives of betta fish. When separated, they didn't chew on their plastic containers. But they did start singing.

Actually, it was more like a murmuring hum.

They hummed tunes I recognized, like Led Zeppelin's 'Stairway to Heaven' and Pink Floyd's 'Breathe'.

Instead of releasing them all into the ocean like we used to, I allowed them some swim time in the old swimming pool in the backyard. Every Sunday, from noon to one, I'd allow them out for playtime, a quick dip in a bigger space.

They tolerated the pool's higher chlorine level as if they were born to it. The pool always looked cleaner after their swim; they licked the walls and the pool bottom while they swam.

By then I'd reduced my collection to less than a dozen because they'd each grown to the size of a baby seal. I had one of each incredible colour. The blue one, the colour of lapis lazuli, always tried to get her way. Her icy blue skin matched the foam bubbles I added to the water. The yellow and green mermaids liked to hold hands and swim together. The yellow one had golden-coloured skin with daffodil-yellow hair, eyes, and tail. The green one had a kind of moss for hair growing in a single stripe. A different species, I guessed. The orange one reminded me of a massive goldfish. She hid under the pool toys and gnawed on the floating mattress, unable to enjoy the freedom of the pool. The red one was as bright as the eyes of a red-eyed tree frog, but acted like a ruby-coloured demon. She made me the most nervous. If given the chance, she liked to nip.

I lured them back into their bins with old, leftover cat treats.

After two years, we were back to three people living in the house. Dylan, my boyfriend, had moved in too. He worked a late shift in the deli and meat section of a supermarket in the city. After cleaning up at work, he usually got in past midnight, bringing any spare meaty titbits home for the mermaids.

My sister had broken up with her husband and returned. I didn't tell her I still kept mermaids in the shed I'd added near the pool.

When I finally let Taryn in on my secret, I'd hoped the reveal would turn out to become a pleasant pastime for her. After all, she'd enjoyed the mermaids as a kid. Instead, Taryn freaked out—said she didn't like fish, especially not half-human-looking fish. She remembered the 'tropical fish' from childhood as trauma-inducing, and agreed to tolerate my collection as long as I kept them in the bins in the shed where she couldn't see them. I hadn't shown her how big they'd grown this time, and decided I never would after she said that if she found any in the shower they'd find themselves slipping down the drain, along with the silverfish, spiders, hair, and odd bobby pins that occasionally sloshed their way down.

This frightened me. I knew my sister could be mean. She'd always had quite the temper, but now, because of her ex, she hated everything in the universe. His very existence put her in a bad mood. But soon my angst had a new source — my neighbour had begun to tie her two barking, tumour-ridden dogs in her backyard during the day.

Basset hounds.

The mermaids couldn't bear the sound of the constant barking; they stressed. *We* stressed. And the rising stress levels both inside and outside the house began to discolour us all.

Luckily, my sister had enough sleeping pills and anti-anxiety medication to calm a pack of hyenas.

I quickly figured out that a few meatballs, each stuffed with half a sleeping pill and tossed over the fence, worked nicely for a while.

One day I left some meat Dylan brought home inside the shed, sitting in the same old Tupperware bowl we used years ago to free the first batches of mermaids. I'd intended to feed the mermaids, but the neighbour's bloody Basset hounds found their way over to my yard and munched up the raw hamburger.

The dogs stood at the pool's edge woofing at the mermaids. Their incessant barking alerted me, and I tried to shoo them back to their yard, but the mermaids in the pool started singing to the crazed hounds. The dogs sang back and were so attracted, they plopped themselves into the pool.

Basset hounds don't do doggy paddle.

One, and then another, went under.

I leapt into the pool, but the mermaids ate up those dogs so quickly that I found myself surrounded by bits of floating doggy fur and bones. Somehow I stayed calm, climbed out, grabbed the pool skimmer, and removed every floating bit that I could identify as dog. I didn't have time to deal with the mermaids and left them in the pool. There wasn't much left of the dogs, but I packed up what remained, and drove it a block over, to a neighbour's garbage cans.

Back home, I asked Taryn if she had any extra anti-anxiety medication.

That night, I woke up about an hour after midnight to the sound of rowdy yelling in the front yard. I peeked between the curtains. My sister's crazy drunken ex had come over with his new girlfriend. They stripped off their clothes on the front lawn, then went round back, probably to dive buck-naked into the pool. I crept quietly through the house and out to the backyard.

Taryn's ex was in the pool thrashing at the water, trying to get out. The mermaids did their best to devour the beast of a man, but finishing off a two-hundred-fifty-pound former linebacker proved to be a bit much, even for them.

I was freaking out and didn't know what to do because, by the time I got to the pool's edge, the only piece of person I could identify was the girlfriend's floating blonde braid.

But Taryn knew what to do.

"You got any of those big coolers we used for picnics at the beach hanging around? The kind with wheels on them, so they roll."

I could only nod.

It took us the rest of the night to fish out the bits of her ex with the pool skimmer, but it only required one cooler to pack up all his remains.

Before sunrise, Taryn and I drove to the same beach we went to as kids. We rolled our cooler down the sand to the ocean, and yanked our sweatpants up to our knees.

We needed deeper water.

My sweatpants became waterlogged. I pulled them off, set them free. So did Taryn.

We swam far out with the cooler bobbing between us.

"This isn't going to work," I said, treading water. "This thing will be found floating out here, or the tide will bring it in. We're done for." But my sister had disappeared, nowhere to be seen. I turned in jerky circles looking for her, terrified she might be drowning.

"Don't worry," she said, sliding up behind me. Then, like an Olympian, she dove headfirst under the water. I watched as her gorgeous golden-scaled tail broke the surface, its feathery fantail fluke catching the first rays of dawn.

When Taryn resurfaced, she had a reedy bullwhip tangled in her long dark-gold hair—a frilled strand of thick seaweed draped her shoulder. She was naked from the waist up. She opened the cooler lid and tipped the contents into the sea. Then she made a high-pitched keening sound, a mix of humming, trilling, and warbling.

"Taryn?" She looked wild.

"Bring them. The ones from home," she said. When she spoke in her strange, gargling voice, I could see all the points on her teeth.

One of her ex's fingers floated toward me and I swooshed it away with a splash of water. Something else bumped my feet. Whether it was a chunk of Taryn's ex or a shark, the surprise of it made me pee.

The last thing I saw, in the morning's bright light, was a swirl of flowing golden hair and the flick of a golden tail above the water's surface—and the floating finger getting snatched away.

It took me until midnight of the following day to load up all of the mermaids in the shed and release them into the ocean. When I got to the beach with the very last of them—a ruby-red beauty—I fell to the sand, exhausted. She'd grown beyond the limits of her bin, and her tail and hair had dragged in the driveway as I hauled her out to the old Valiant.

The full moon gave me much-needed light, but not the strength to haul the bin into deep water. I backed the car onto the beach and hoped I wouldn't get stuck.

At the water's softly lapping edge, I dumped her out. Ruby flopped onto the wet sand and lay there, glistening red in the moon's light. After a few seconds, she moved a little, made the same singsong keening vibration I'd heard Taryn make. It grew loud and piercing—not a comfortable sensation.

I heard heavy splashing in the deep, dark waters beyond the shore.

In the line of moonlight painted across the ocean's surface, hundreds of mermaids were gathered, their heads bobbing above the small waves. They keened, and Ruby revived, finding the strength she needed. I followed behind her. While I stood ankle-deep, Ruby pushed hard against the wet sand with her powerful arms. She gripped the beach with her talon hands, snaked her powerful tail once, twice, then pushed into the black sea.

Their heads bobbed on the swells like the round silhouettes of seals but for the triangular veil formed by their long glittery hair floating out behind them on the water's surface. I searched for Taryn, called her name, but the keening was loud, growing louder, a sound like no other. It made me think of the wheels of a train squealing against steel rails in the night. Taryn had gone with them.

The pain of their song hurt me. The sound stabbed through my head, my heart, down into my groin, my legs. So agonizing was this rapid pulse of hot steel firing through my abdomen that it felled me, sent me screaming and crying into the frigid deep water. The cold ocean soothed my hot agony. I lay there, unable to rise. I tried moving my legs but a flash of gold in the moonlight blinded me. I released my hair from its braid and combed my fingers through until my mane floated around me, a wild halo as the tide gently rocked me out to sea. I remembered Ruby's strength and determination, and imitated it. I followed the singing, humming, murmuring that was somehow both familiar and unknown.

I joined the school in the streak of moonlight; joined my sisters who gobbled plastic like sea otters feasting on oysters. I saw the cooler and plastic bin on the beach, wished to chew on it, eat it away, but there was no returning to the shore now.

We were ten thousand strong, and the ocean needed us, needed our appetite to devour all things deadly — to us, to the sea, to our mother.

FEATURE INTERVIEW

Rhea Rose

Pulp Literature: *There's nothing quite like summertime for a glorious (and gory) mermaid story. Tell us about the inspiration for 'A Collection of Secrets'.*

Rhea Rose: I've written a mermaid poem, but I've always wanted to write a mermaid story! But I know mermaids are popular, and many stories are written about them. When writing about popular creatures, a writer wants a new twist, a new lens through which to experience them. As a kid, I ordered sea monkeys from a comic book, but they never arrived. A friend told me (or may have shown me) that they were actually 'shrimp dust' that, when poured into water, grew into tiny, wormy shrimps. I don't even know if that's true, but the seed of the idea for this story came from that memory. What if the sea monkeys grew and turned out to be mermaids? I wanted *my* mermaids to have agency and power, be a force for the planet, and get some payback for the damage done to their world from polluting plastics. I wanted them to be more than sexy sirens.

PL: *On the surface (forgive the pun), 'A Collection of Secrets' is a fun romp to the land of mermaids and childhood curiosity. But along the way, we find ourselves in the depths of consumption and environmental spoilage. What do you see are our responsibilities to this planet?*

RR: A question that causes me great conflict. On the one hand, I know we are responsible for keeping the planet safe and clean. On the other hand, we all indulge in everyday things that hurt our world's natural resources. I don't want to see plastics in the stomachs of wildlife, yet I use and dispose of plastics all the time. Of course, if there's a nonplastic, non-polluting option, I use it instead. The very least we can do is be aware of our footprint and keep it as light as possible. Public pressure on the fast-everything industry is a must; if they have to reduce profits to use something other than plastic, then do it. I'm very glad to see electric cars (which should have happened a few decades earlier), water, wind, and solar power — all good — but in reality, every technology created brings its own problems to the planet. Unless we're all willing to go back to a simple mechanical age, we will have to work hard by holding accountable those industries that do the most damage, to keep the planet free of toxins.

PL: *We published your modern folktale 'The Gamogue' in Issue 12, Autumn 2016. What has changed for you as a writer, whether it be the themes you explore or your process itself, since then?*

RR: In the past, I've always considered myself a science fiction writer, whether in writing fiction or poetry, but more and more, I find myself writing what I'd call dark literary fantasy. I've always had a deep calling to include children in my work, without writing children's stories. I like exploring children's resilience, versatility, and creativity under challenging situations. I loved being a child and always wished I could stay in that land. The rules are different for children. At times I like to go back to explore their world. These days, markets look for ecology-related themes, whether they specify it or not, so I try to include that in my work, if possible. I've found I've had to be more aware of what's on the horizon for themes. Whereas in the past, I wrote what interested me, now I combine market needs with my interests. These days I'm drawn to horror and poetry. I've gone back to the well of poetry — a place I go when I'm looking to recharge my writing mojo. I'm writing both long and short these days: longer fiction (like novellas and novels) and shorter poetry, which gives me less time for short stories. But I love writing short stories and won't leave them behind. One thing that has changed is the humour that has started to creep into almost everything I'm writing. I love comedy, and it's started to become a part of my style.

PL: *As a writer of both speculative fiction and poetry, how do you find each informs the writing of the other?*

RR: That's an interesting question. It doesn't, at least not on the surface. There might be similar themes, but I don't think about my poetry informing my short stories or the other way around. My speculative writing is informed by my interest in highlighting what I find interesting as an observer of people, life, the effects of science and technology, and what goes on in the shadows. As a writer of poetry and shorts, I can only say that I have a sense of producing either a poem or short story at the time of writing. I get a feeling, an urge, a longing just before writing. I've thought about turning poetry into short fiction but have never done it, though I have turned short stories into longer works. I'm careful when writing prose fiction because I begin to rhyme and become rhythmic in my paragraphs.

When you talk to folks about music, you'll find some are *music* listeners and some are *lyric* listeners. I love the words and the music of my favourite songs, but I've always sought the words over the musicality. I've always loved the sound, the feelings, of words, and how they carry meaning. These little packets of drawn sticks make a word filled with the juice of thought and feeling that deliver all we know in the universe. My dad wrote a lot of poetry and recited poetry at home. His memory was astounding. I wrote poetry to impress him, the way he impressed me with his poetry. He also wrote stories. I tried to emulate him in the two genres. My poetry comes from a deeper consciousness, a more difficult place to analyze than the place the stories come from. No doubt they inform one another, but I trust the system and don't think about it too much.

PL: *What are your yet-to-tell stories?*

RR: I have some dark fairy tales I'm working on and a gothic-horror/science-fiction tale. I've recently become obsessed with the hare and rabbit, and know I've got some stories to tell with these critters. I have some longer works (novels and scripts) I want to get back to. And I want to write much more poetry. I'm working on a historical *Secret Garden*-type story. It's a story I'd really like to be inside of. I always have something going, but most of it doesn't see the light of day.

PL: *Where are your favourite places to write?*

RR: I'm in my happy place when no one is home, and I can make tea and turn on music or something else for white noise (I love to have a favourite movie playing on the television), while I'm in a nearby room, writing with my laptop on my lap. I do have a home office, and once I get settled in there, I like to write in that office, but going there takes a bit more effort. Something about first entering an office space doesn't feel conducive to creativity. I've tried coffee shops, but I find people watching way too distracting. I sometimes go to a study stall in the library, but that's a very lonely feeling. I love to write in hotel rooms! I like to be alone — but not lonely — while I write. My guilty little secret: I like to write in bed, late at night when the world is asleep.

PL: *As the editor of* Polar Starlight: Magazine of Canadian Speculative Poetry *(and with my apologies to Rilke), what words of advice would you include in your letters to a young speculative poet?*

RR: Oh, no pressure! Okay, to the young speculative fiction writer: You are ablaze with a wild magic. It lives inside you — a searing pool of beauty, horror, confounding mystery — your creativity is a golden stag in the forest of story. Call to your wild creative magic through ritual, dance, prayer, and honour it by giving it form with your words. You're a young hunter; with practice, your aim improves, and your words will hit the beating heart.

PL: *Who are your writing mentors? What is the most helpful advice you have received? Which 'rules' have you learned are better left broken?*

RR: Honestly, I can't think of any single rule better left *unbroken*. I always break all the rules (and editors often bring me back from the brink!), and so do other writers, like the rule of show don't tell. Show whenever possible. But it's not always possible to show, especially for backstory. Yes, use flashbacks if you're skilled at this. And if you practise — and read what other writers do — you find breaking that rule is possible. Expositions can be written in interesting or exciting ways. In poetry, you can break all the rules, but I think the challenge is keeping *some* rules when writing poetry. I don't like poetry with no punctuation or left untitled. I prefer to see some use of those rules-as-tools in poetry.

PL: *What do you see are the latest or emerging trends in speculative fiction and poetry?*

RR: Writing speculative fiction and poetry used to be a fun, guilty little secret! These days, everybody is writing speculative, and as a result, it's become a more serious endeavour. More markets are open to it. There is more pay. In terms of themes and trends, I see a trend toward strong women as main characters — superwomen, super smart, super strong in many cases. And toward non-white characters and non-European-centric stories. As I mentioned, climate change and offshoots of climate change, like corporate disrespect for the planet, presented as a 'bad guy', is trending. A character with an anti-LGBTQ attitude may also be considered a 'bad guy' scenario in fiction. Horror is enjoying a renaissance, and I see gaming having a huge influence on publication in the world of science fiction. The poetry market has also opened up and pays well in many cases, sometimes as much for a poem as a short story. Submissions to *Polar Starlight* include an overabundance of alien-contact poetry. In some ways, the alien is the last frontier of the Other, in writing about strange and unfamiliar beings and situations. At this time, there's no cultural appropriation when writing about aliens!

PL: *Who were your biggest influences, literary or otherwise? Which books and authors do you return to again and again?*

RR: I spent many summers reading and rereading the Lord of the Rings trilogy before it became popular (in the media). I love the language and adventure of the characters in that land. I remember being disappointed when Tom Bombadil, one of my favourite characters, was left out of the movie. As a kid, I loved Dickens, and now I go back to read quotes and sections of his novels online. When I was young, I loved stories with imaginative ideas and stories with the underdog kid. I spent summers with the Dune novels (until they became media fodder). I also loved *The Secret Garden* and still keep a copy of it where I can see it. I find Shakespeare always inspiring, and while I don't read the whole plays, I often go to sections of his work for inspiration, and I attend Bard on the Beach. Shakespeare always gets the human condition right — except for some of his interpretations of women! While I don't write historical fiction (though I am attempting it in my 'Secret Garden' story, and it might be argued that 'A Collection of Secrets' is somewhat historical), I loved Pauline Gedge's novels and Eileen Kernaghan's work. The latter writes some of the best speculative poetry. I must have their books on my bookshelves to feel secure as a writer. For many years I went to William Gibson's work for a sense of science fiction. I still refer to these works when I'm trying to achieve an ambiance or even a style in a piece I'm writing. I look at diction, pacing, stuff like that. The most helpful advice I've received is to 'write what you'd like to read'. If I stick to that single piece of advice, I can always find my way out of the chaos and overwhelm which can ensue when writing through a piece, especially something longer. Recently (which to me is in the last five to ten years, lol), I read an interview with Margaret Atwood, who said writers should be writing about climate change. I keep that in the back of my mind when making writing choices. I also love movies! I love action adventure movies like *Jurassic Park*, even though I don't usually read in that area. I love studying what the writers have done in the script and guessing what direction a storyline must go.

PL: *What books are on your to-be-read pile?*

RR: That's a big pile, and with Audible and Kindle adding to it, the pile just grows and grows. I like to do long walks, so Audible is great for keeping up on the booklist. It's more challenging to find time to read. My eyes get tired more quickly these days so it's always a juggling game—read or write until the eyes can't take anymore. I love reading how-to-write books! Tim Waggoner's *Writing in the Dark* and others always have little gems I like to try. I find these books inspirational. In fiction, I'm reading a book called *Leech* by Hiron Ennes, which I got free at Stokercon 2022. I chose it because it's gothic science fiction/horror, and I'm currently writing a gothic/science fiction/horror story. I'm trying to write a more modern story, and this book reminds me of the rules of the gothic genre. The main character has several personalities 'living' inside it, and their POVs are presented while the main character is going about his business. It's a classic trapped-in-an-old-European-chateau-with-a-frightening-baron-as-your-boss situation.

I'm also reading fiction books that are page-turners, like Ruth Ware's *The Turn of the Key*, learning what these authors do to create riveting fiction. I'm just finishing *Jade City* by Fonda Lee, and I've got Kelley Armstrong's latest books, *A Stitch in Time* and *Wolf's Bane*, on my to-be-read list. I've been rereading fairy tales from *The Blue Fairy Book* by Andrew Lang, and stories from *Sword Stone Table* by Swapna Krishna and Jenn Northington. I read in bite-sized pieces, unless I'm walking and listening to a book. I also have a list of literary books. I'm reading *Poetry Showcase Volume III*, edited by Stephanie M Wytovich and published by Horror Writers Association, and *Mexican Gothic* by Silvia Moreno-Garcia. And the list goes on!

PL: *As we all begin again, what words of advice would the 2022 Rhea have for the 2019 Rhea?*

RR: Ha-ha. Well, I'd say, "Pace yourself, bring your writing to the forefront, no need to backburner anymore, and trust the process. Remember, you're writing for *you*, and if others find joy and interest in what you're doing, bonus!" I quit writing every day! Every day, I think, I've said, "I'm done, no more!" And then I find myself at the keyboard, poking around at something, and next thing you know, I'm writing again.

PL: *Thank you for speaking with us. Before we go, tell us: what are you working on now?*

RR: I want to thank you and all the folks at *Pulp Literature* for your support of me as a writer, and for the great publication you put out. It's a wonderful place for writers to publish, and it's very supportive of writers.

I'm working on two things, a novel (surprise! lol), working title: *Industrial Gothic*, a science fiction/horror story set in Vancouver, and on a longish short story (it might be a novelette or a novella) called 'The Gladiator's Garden', a dark fantasy very loosely based on the fairy tale titled 'The Princess On The Glass Hill'. I've recently written poetry for a composer I collaborate with, and he puts my words to music. I will continue to do that for as long as he needs poetry. And of course, I work on other poetry pieces all the time. *Polar Starlight* magazine has been so successful, and I hope to eventually include more reviews of works of speculative poetry. Perhaps I will seek funding to pay writers more. We'll see. I've promised myself to make my work a priority!

Selected Bibliography

'Riddle of the Sphinx Revisited', in *On Spec* #117, September 2021

Earthrise 2021, Nicholas Kelly musical composition, lyrics by Rhea Rose

Stellar Evolutions, ed. Rhea Rose, 2020

'Venus and the Milky Way', in *Triangulation: Dark Skies*, eds. Diane Turnshek and Chloe Nightingale, 2018

'Gel Theta One' and 'From Alpha Centauri the Earth is a Blue Bowl of Fish Soup', in *Compostela*, eds. Spider Robinson and James Alan Gardner, 2017

'The Gamogue', in *Pulp Literature* Issue 12, Autumn 2016

'Bones of Bronze, Limbs Like Iron', in *Clockwork Canada*, ed. Dominik Parisien, 2016

'Scar Tissue' (cowritten with Colleen Anderson), in *Second Contacts*, eds. Michael Rimar and Hayden Trenholm, 2015

Pandora's Progeny, RainWood Press, 2012

GWANNYN'S SONG

JM Landels

JM Landels *is the author of the bestselling* Allaigna's Song *trilogy, the final book of which,* Allaigna's Song: Chorale, *is coming soon from Pulp Literature Press. 'Gwannyn's Song' tells the story of Allaigna's grandfather's second wife, Gwannyn Doristi. When asked why she chose to write this piece, Jen told us, "Gwannyn was cast in the role of wicked stepmother against her will. She wanted me to tell her true story." Reader beware: here there be spoilers. You can find @jmlandels on most social media platforms and at jmlandels.stiffbunnies.com.*

GWANNYN'S SONG

It has been a colder than usual winter, and the late Bera wind that blows up the river Krone chills Gwannyn Doristi's reddened nose and cheeks, bringing stinging tears to her eyes.

She should have no more tears left in her. She thought she had wept them all in the two clearmoons since her mother, the Kingfisher Queen, and her red-eyed father, the Royal Consort, accepted the formal offer of Chanist Brandis's hand. Her sister Cyrnan, twelve years her senior, stroked her hair as Gwannyn cried onto her shoulder.

"He is a good man, Gwannyn, kind and handsome."

"And he loves another."

Cyrnan nodded. "And he has set her aside for the good of the nations. Do you think it was easy for him? I've seen the looks those two share across the dinner table. He was foolish to marry a Leisanmira, but he has taken the brave step to correct his folly."

Cyrnan pulled away and held her little sister at arm's length. "You must be as brave as he. Did you think that because you are not Mother's heir you could marry as you please? Naz is a commoner—Mother would never approve. Be thankful you've made a match with a handsome prince—of Brandishear, no less—rather than with one of our dreadful dukes."

Gwannyn has made the most of her time since then.

The wind lessens as she descends into the shelter of Caella's lower streets, and she pats her face dry, warming already as Nazzedh's workshop at the bottom of Rose Alley comes into view.

Gwannyn rolls over, resting her head in the hollow of Naz's shoulder. Her fingers trace the damp line of curly hair that points towards his navel, drawing patterns in the wet semen on his belly. The two of them are careful, as always. But how she wishes they didn't have to be. If for once they could remain joined. *Not just for once,* she amends. *Forever.*

She brings her leg across his hips and buries her face in his armpit, biting her lip to stop from crying. The smell of his sweat is intoxicating and only makes her sadder. Her tears refuse to be held back any longer.

"Gwannyn, love." Naz rolls to face her and strokes hair out of her eyes. "Was it as bad as that?" He smiles, kissing her nose.

So she tells him. She didn't mean to. She wanted to spare him this pain and keep their last few weeks together unchanged. But, of course, *she* is not unchanged.

He runs through, in swift order, all the thoughts and feelings she has already experienced. Shock, protest, anger, grief, and scheming.

"Let us flee," he suggests, as if she hadn't thought of it.

"And live how? Your clients, your loom, are here." Naz was the finest weaver in all of Caella—perhaps all of Elalantar.

"I have clients across the Ilmar. I can set up a loom anywhere there's a port."

"And your work is instantly recognizable. As am I. There is nowhere we could go and not be found."

The afternoon sun coming through the high windlet of his back room is almost flat, which means the dinner hour is near and she will be missed soon.

"I would work forever as a farmer," he persists. "Or a wood-cutter, or delve the mines. I don't need to be a weaver." He pulls his breeks on. "But I could never force you to live that life."

She gives a humourless laugh. "What do I care for this comfortable life if it is without love?" She wipes her face on the hem of her shift before slipping it over her head. "But I cannot deprive my country of the alliance it needs. I will sail to Rheran and wed this Prince, and when he kisses me to seal our vows, I'll close my eyes and think of you." As she says it, her chin trembles, and tears threaten again. "Duty is the price I owe for the privilege I've been born to."

Naz gathers her into his arms. "There must be another choice."

"If there was, don't you think I'd take it?" She has to stand on her tiptoes to kiss his beautiful mouth. "But I will enjoy every last moment I can with you until then."

Three days later, Gwannyn pauses outside an unassuming wooden door. It is set below the level of the street and crowded between the grander façades of spice merchants' and vintners' storefronts. It is an odd location for a mage to set up shop. She knocks, waits, waits some more, and turns to leave, relieved. What is she, some lovesick girl visiting a potion-seller to cure her heartache?

Her foot is upon the step to go back up to the street when a voice says, "Enter."

She stays there a moment more, hovering on the stair between the busy street and the low door before stepping back down.

The room is dark, lit only by a single half-spent taper in the centre of a square table. Despite the dim light, Gwannyn keeps the hood of her cloak well over her head. The woman opposite her is cowled as well, with only her lips and chin showing in the flickering light.

"Close the door," the woman says. Her voice is young, as are the hands that gesture to the empty chair nearest the door. "Please," she says, and sits across the table.

Gwannyn isn't superstitious—she doesn't believe that fortune tellers can trade fates and alter destinies. But when her maid Parine, her confidante since childhood and the woman she trusts most in the world, suggested the mage who runs the apothecary on Cornmill Street, Gwannyn allowed herself hope. Perhaps the mage could give her a potion to help her love her husband-to-be and lessen the pain of forsaking Naz. Money is no object to a princess of the realm. Perhaps she can buy a balm for Naz's heart as well.

The woman seems to know why she is here.

"Do you truly want to forget your love?"

Taken aback, Gwannyn stammers, "No. I …" She swallows the ever-present sadness that lurks beneath her surface. "I just want the pain to stop. For both of us."

"Life is pain," the mage says. "Death is the only way to stop it. If I take the pain, you would lose the memories—all the joy you've felt. And that is a different kind of pain." She waits a breath, and when Gwannyn stays silent, continues. "But if you're sure, it can be done. I would need to cast the working on you both."

That would entail revealing Naz's identity and making him complicit in magic of questionable legality. Would he agree to lose his memories of her? And could she bear to lose hers?

"Is there no other way?"

"There is, but it is long and costly."

"Price is no object."

The woman's full lips broaden slightly, and she lifts the cowl from a face and head so like Gwannyn's own that it is like looking in a mirror.

"Why seven?" asked Naz. "Don't mistake me—I will wait for you forever. But why seven years?"

"It is a good length for a marriage. Time enough to give him heirs and see they are well started in life."

"And will you want to leave them, and him, by then?"

She took his hands. "You are my one true love, Naz. All others will be like candles to the sun."

If her wedding trunks are larger than warranted, none remark upon it. A royal marriage is cause for extravagance. It is not till several months after she is settled into the royal apartments that she locks her dressing room door behind her and opens the final chest that made the journey from Elalantar to Brandishear with her.

The mirror is wrapped in layers of soft velvet and sits at the top of the chest. She takes it out, struggling with the weight as she lays it, wrappings and all, on the dressing table. This is not a task she can call servants to aid her in, nor can she ask her husband for help. The two legs come out next, almost as heavy as the looking glass itself. They feel as if they could be solid gold, though further examination reveals that the ornate legs, worked to look like a pair of raptor's feet, have steel rods in the centre to support the weight of the glass. She attaches them to the crossbar, grateful for easy-turning screws that obviate the need for tools.

When the leg assembly is complete, she unwraps the mirror at last and settles it onto its holder. She imagines a tingle running through her hands and forearms, but the mirror is just a mirror, showing her face and the clothes hanging behind her, nothing more.

There is more in the chest: a smaller bundle of velvet. As she unwraps it, the evenlamp sends spears of light from between her fingers around the small room, and the plain silver ring on her right little finger glows in answer. She replaces the evenlamp in the wall sconce with this new one, which has no trigger word marked upon it nor any shutter to turn it off. This time, when she reaches towards the mirror, her silver ring thrums, and the glass darkens and ripples.

She waits, and waits some more, her heart pounding ever louder as panic rises within her. "Naz," she whispers, then calls louder, "Naz!"

Had they lied? The mirror, ring, and evenlamp are clearly ensorcelled. What is she missing that would allow her to see her love?

"Naz," she calls again, her lips nearly touching the darkened mirror, her breath fogging the glass. "Are you there?"

At last a speck of light appears in the dark centre of the mirror. She stops herself from reaching out to touch it. It is a door opening. And through it comes a man holding an evenlamp to match her own. But he is not Naz. This man's skin is darker— nearly as black as the mirror— and his close-cropped hair is greying above the ears.

"You're late," he says without preamble. "And early."

"Who are you?" she demands, forcing the tremble from her chin. "Where is Nazzedh?"

"The appointed hour is midday," he continues as if she hadn't spoken. "And you should have engaged the mirror weeks ago."

It was true. They told her to make contact as soon as she was married. But she needed to immerse herself in Brandishear, and Chanist, first. If she had seen Naz in those early weeks, she would have fled in the night and returned to Elalantar, consequences be damned.

The noon bells ring across the Bastion. "It is midday," she insists, refusing to justify herself to this stranger.

The man leans close. "Where you are, noon comes an hour earlier."

Chastened, she waits, and makes excuses to Chanist, who is expecting her for their afternoon walk. Pregnancy sickness has long since left her, but she pleads it anyway, and takes to her bed. She finds she is genuinely sad to miss her walk with Chanist. Sometimes their strolls take them through the castle gardens or on the wall-walk of the Bastion, but more often of late they take a path through the city, accompanied by a pair of knights who follow three paces behind them. In this companionable fashion they explore the neighbourhoods of Rheran in its spring garb of pale green and new blossoms.

"Just wait till summer," Chanist told her proudly as they walked through Princes Square for the first time. "The city is a paradise of riotous flowers and sweet fruits."

It is a far cry from the orderly conifers that line Caella's broad, straight streets and carpet Elalantar's shores from Farwiel to Elistal. She misses the smell of the cool, wet forests of the coast and the rich farmlands that surround her home. Elalantar supplies almost all the wheat and barley, and most of the timber and wool, for the entire Ilmar. Which is why her union with Chanist is so vital. But she could also grow to love the opulent warmth of Rheran, with its vibrant theatres, excellent wine, abundant fruit, and clever artisans. But there is one artisan still who occupies the largest room in her heart.

"We'll walk tomorrow," she promises her husband. "I would like to see the commons outside the city."

He bends over and kisses her forehead as she lies curled on her side. "Can I bring you anything?"

She brings a hand to her mouth, feigning nausea, and shakes her head. "I just need a nap," she says.

"Then I'll leave you be." His hand runs down her shoulder and stops at her waist, which is already thickening. A bright tenderness appears in his eyes — the same light she sees every time her stepdaughter Lauresa enters the room. *At least he loves children,* she thinks, praying that the child she carries resembles her.

When the interminable hour is over, she returns to her garderobe and waves the ring in front of the mirror again. Fear grips her when the mirror fails to respond, until she remembers to unwrap the evenlamp once more.

This time it is Zaradne, the mage she met in Caella when the wheels of this mad scheme began to roll.

"Hello, Zara," the woman in the mirror says to her.

Gwannyn blinks, confused, till she remembers the agreement. "Good afternoon, Gwannyn."

"I think 'Your Highness' would be more appropriate, and easier for you, don't you agree?"

Gwannyn swallows her pride and dips her head. "Your Highness," she agrees, and then lifts her gaze again to look the woman in her soft brown eyes. "Where is Naz?"

Zara smiles. "You will see him shortly. But first, we have much to catch up. Why did you wait so long?"

Gwannyn dissembles. "It took longer than I had expected to have this room appointed." Over the coming years she will have to expose all her inmost thoughts and feelings to this changeling in the mirror. But not today.

Zara seems to accept her explanation at face value. "Well, this will take some time, then. Less in the future, if we talk weekly—or better, daily."

Over seven years, the mirror becomes both Gwannyn's friend and her enemy. It shows her glimpses of her beloved Naz, alive and well through the ups and downs of an artist with an ascending star. But far more hours are spent revealing every aspect of her life to Zara—from the quotidian, to the political, to the most intimate.

At first the betrayals seem small: she can easily trade a detail from her wedding night or gossip about a courtier as part of her bargain. And in some ways, it is comforting to have a confidante in those early days far from home. But the better Zara knows her, the more strings she has to pull at Gwannyn's heart and mind. Gwannyn seems unable to withhold information—Zara always knows when she dissembles. And there are hints, never spoken outright, that imply that the well-being of Naz, and later her children and even Chanist, are tied to Gwannyn's continued cooperation.

And Zara, always similar to her in appearance, has grown to adopt Gwannyn's voice and mannerisms so impeccably that

Gwannyn sometimes feels she is indeed talking to herself in the mirror.

Two months before the seventh anniversary of her wedding to Chanist, Zara asks her, "Our favourite dressmaker—the one on Arandh Street—do we trust her?"

Maids and dressmakers will be the hardest to fool, Gwannyn knows—harder even than husband and children—so the question makes sense.

"She knows my shape better than any. I would rather we stop seeing her than any harm should befall her." Maids are easily replaced, and she has never kept any on for more than a year. But good dressmakers are hard to find.

Zara shakes her head. "If she is trustworthy, she will have a commission that will set her up for life." The woman in the mirror smiles softly. "Tell me, should we give it to her, or to your second favourite?"

Gwannyn swallows, unable to hope at the unspoken meaning of this exchange. "To her," she says, but her mind is whirring away elsewhere. "Does this mean ... ?"

Zara nods. "Two moons, it should take, more or less. The dressmaker will receive the cloth and the commission. When it is done, here's what you will do ..."

When the plain black cloak arrives, Gwannyn is sitting with Chanist in the solar. She is no mage, but the cloak feels sticky with magic, even through its wrapping of linen.

"What is that, my dear?" asks Chanist over his morning cup of ale.

"A new cloak from my dressmaker."

"May I see?" he asks. "She does excellent work."

"Not now, love." Gwannyn swats his hand away. "Your fingers are greasy from breakfast, and it's just a cloak."

She feels sorrow immediately for her words and actions, but he shrugs and drains his ale, then kisses her on the top of the head and leaves to dress for the day. Gwannyn stays several moments longer, staring at the parcel in her lap. If it means what she thinks it does, she should be happy. But she is terrified.

Tonight, Gwannyn does what she has not in seven years: she covers the mirror with the heavy velvet cloth it came wrapped in. The room seems darker and smaller without it, despite the evenlamp that never leaves its sconce.

She drapes the black cloak around her shoulders. In the main chamber, Chanist sleeps heavily, the haze of his brandied breath hovering over the bed. She bends over to give him a kiss, but stops herself. As fond as she has grown, she cannot afford to be sentimental.

Wrapped in the glamour-encrusted cloak, she walks out past guards and servants still awake beyond midnight, and not a soul notices her. Will anyone? she wonders, both hoping and fearing that there is some unique part of her that Zara can't replicate.

Never has she walked unescorted through the city she now thinks of as hers. But she is in no danger, for the cloak's glamour blends with the shadows. She slips past the night watchmen at the docks and walks softly down the western pier, a dark ghost in the thin moonlight. At the end of the pier is a figure cloaked in shimmering cloth. Even though the clearmoon bleaches the figure of colour, she can tell the cloak is rainbow-hued and beautiful beyond measure. She has seen it on Naz's loom, in glimpses.

"Naz?" she asks, not daring to breathe.

The figure drops the hood and Gwannyn exhales. Of course not.

"Well met, sister," Zara says, and embraces Gwannyn.

Gwannyn returns the gesture mechanically, feeling none of the implied warmth. "I have waited seven years. I have kept my end of the bargain and more. Where is Naz?"

Zara smiles. "A ship will dock at this berth tomorrow at noon. Your Naz will be aboard."

Gwannyn's shoulders begin to shake. "And then?"

"And then you will be free to live the life you've always wanted."

Burdened with unshed tears, she planned to walk straight out from the castle, blinkered to the life she was leaving behind. Yet she cannot help but hear her children's voices, raised in laughter, floating up from the garden. She stops, and instead of continuing toward the front gates, takes the stairs down to the sunken garden. Lauresa is playing the ogre, back turned as her young half siblings sneak up on her. She whirls around, and Perran, Miani, and Phelan flee for the safety of the berry bushes, shrieking. Lauresa catches Perran and tickles her ferociously.

Gwannyn stays half-hidden in the stairwell, loath to interrupt their happiness. Will they know? Will this be the last truly happy day they have? She shakes her head at her own self-importance. Lauresa lost her mother, and yet here she is, a bright and cheerful adolescent who clearly loves her siblings. Gwannyn's own mother was hardly a nurturing figure, too busy ruling a principality to have time for her children. And yet Gwannyn felt her youth was happy, bathed in the love of her nurse, her father, and her sister. Until she was torn away from her home for a marriage of state.

Gwannyn has tried to raise Lauresa as if she were her own. She thinks she has succeeded. She must trust Zara will do the same for all four.

She said her silent goodbyes to all of them when she put them to bed last night, but she is pulled back to them like an oarless boat on the tide. She removes her cloak and drops it, with her pack, at the foot of the stairs. "Darlings," she calls as she sweeps into the garden, opening her arms wide.

"Mama!" Phelan squeaks and runs to her, followed by his two older sisters.

She kneels and envelops the three of them in her arms one last time, and her heart breaks.

She won't do it. She can't. However much she once loved Naz, she loves them a hundred times more. She will greet Naz, and spend the afternoon with him, then wish him fond farewell, releasing him from his vow. He waited seven years — she can ask no more than that.

Lauresa is watching her, head cocked to one side. "What's wrong?" Lauresa asks.

Gwannyn's chained heart wrenches and floats free as she takes hold of the rudder of her life. "Nothing. Nothing is wrong, my dears," she says, and she truly feels it for the first time in seven years. "I'm going into town. Would you like me to bring a treat from Herron's?"

Lauresa is the only one old enough to be puzzled by Gwannyn's strange behaviour, but all she says is, "Lemon drops would be nice."

The others clamour agreement, and she leaves them to their game, her heart light.

"**Where is he?**" The lightness in her heart rushes out of her when she sees Zara alone on the dock.

"On board," Zara says, with that mirror-image smile, holding out her hand. "Come." Zara walks halfway up the gangplank of the small cog that is moored there.

Gwannyn follows to the foot of the plank. "Send him out, please."

Zara shakes her head. "We will trade cloaks within the cabin, not out here on the wharf."

"There is no need. I'm staying." A breath of icy wind whips in from the water and blows Gwannyn's hood back. "Let me see him again. We will take our lunch at the Anchor tavern, and I will release him from his vow, and you from your debt."

Zara reaches out, touches Gwannyn's face tenderly. "Of course," she says, her eyes full of sympathy. Zara's other hand opens, and the wind blows a puff of powder into Gwannyn's face.

Gwannyn blinks, tastes the sickly sweet odour as it enters her nostrils. Her eyes water, and she stumbles, grasping Zara's shoulder to steady herself. She feels the other woman's arm slip around her, guiding her up the gangplank. She drags her feet, swaying dangerously close to the edge of the plank and the green water below, but Zara's grip is firm as she steers her through the rail and towards the low door of the stern cabin.

Tears stream down Gwannyn's face, too late to wash the drug from her eyes and nose. Zara removes the plain black cloak from Gwannyn's shoulders and guides her to the bunk, helping her sit. Even that is too much for Gwannyn's murky head. She tumbles over, feeling the bunk catch and hold her. Zara spreads the rainbow cloak over Gwannyn, as tenderly as a mother tucking in her child.

"Bring them lemon drops," Gwannyn says. "I promised them lemon drops."

"Of course." Zara's voice is muffled. "A promise is a promise."

§

For more magic and intrigue set in the lands of the Ilmar, check out the spellbinding conclusion to the Allaigna's Song trilogy, Allaigna's Song: Chorale, *on sale from Pulp Literature Press: pulpliterature.com/product/allaignas-song-chorale/*

TO QI HONG: LOVE LOST & FOUND

Yuan Changming

Yuan Changming *has work in* Best of the Best Canadian Poetry, BestNewPoemsOnline, Poetry Daily, *and elsewhere, across forty-eight countries. Yuan has received twelve Pushcart Prize nominations, and his most recent chapbook is* Limerence. *Yuan has been nominated for, and served on the jury for, Canada's National Magazine Awards. Together with Allen Yuan, he publishes* Poetry Pacific, *found at poetrypacific.blogspot.ca.*

To Qi Hong: Love Lost & Found

1/ Missing in Missed Moments

Each time I miss you
          A bud begins to bloom
     So you are surrounded by flowers
Everywhere you go

Each time I miss you
          A dot of light pops up
     So you are illuminated by a whole sky
Of stars through the night

2/ The Softest Power Ever

What softens
               A human heart is
Neither money nor honey

Rather, it is a good natured smile of
Some dog playing with a cat, a bird

Feeding her young with her broken wings
Covering them against cold rain at noon
The whispering of a zephyr blowing
From nowhere, the mist flirting fitfully
With the copse at twilight, the flower
Trying to outlive its destiny, as well

As the few words you actually meant
To say to her but somehow you forgot
     In the tender of last night

THE TWO OH FOUR SIX

Dustin Moon

Dustin Moon *is a writer from Vancouver Island, BC, with a passion for stories told through the lens of queer characters. His work has appeared in Mischief Media's* A Story Most Queer *and* FreeFall *magazine. He lives in Victoria with his husband and his brand-new puppy, Bramble. Please follow him on Twitter — he thinks he's hilarious on there.*

The Two Oh Four Six

I lingered in Em's driveway despite the late afternoon sun and stared across the hectic road at the three or four (maybe five?) boats that waded around the edge of the to-be-extended breakwater, the walkway cordoned off for construction. Still in geological survey stages. Nobody could answer how an extension to the breakwater was meant to stymie the increasing rise, but city council had dismissed any media questions. And everyone else? Too hot to care. The heat seeped through my dress shirt, so I went inside.

Em bought the place at 2046 Dallas Road in late 2013 — a bargain then, though she didn't know it — but didn't transform it into a speakeasy-in-plain-sight until the pandemic forced the last gay bar in Victoria to shutter. The owners scuttled, and desperation inspired her: she beseeched the city to rezone her property, make it a pub of sorts. The place was already built for it. Designed in the early aughts as an uber-modern plaything for tasteless summer homeowners, the entire upper floor was a long, gaudy bar with a spacious sitting area in the corner and a decent though narrow balcony. The interior was hidden from the busy street by tilted, smoky windows that served a superlative ocean view.

But if you knew Dallas Road, then you knew it was a folly fight to begin with. The city denied Em's request. That picturesque stretch of shoreline drive and opulent, wide-windowed houses, besmirched by a *pub*? (Much less a *gay* pub?) The nimbys protested her application with gumption.

Em shrugged it off. We all did. The idea was only sprung to accommodate the five of us, anyway, maybe the odd invitee. Now, of course, with health ordinances lifted, not just one but *two* new gay bars have grandly opened downtown. We still go to Em's. She bartends, drinks with us, and at the end of each weekend we e-transfer her a share of the liquor and upkeep costs. We are too old for the *real* gay bar scene. We were too old before quarantine.

Benny sat in his usual spot at the short end of the bar. The oldest of our millennial gaggle, he had unofficially dubbed our bar the Society of Ancient Queers. The rest of us stuck with the Two Oh Four Six, though after the drinks overflowed, Benny's lexicon could be infectious. Benny was an accountant for a downtown firm. He lived in a stupidly large penthouse blocks away from his office. He was also afflicted with Permanent Bachelorhood.

Em was behind the bar, hair pinned up, Montreal Canadiens jersey belted tight around her waist with a gem-encrusted buckle. Elton John's 'Amoreena' played at elevator volume from her portable speaker. Behind her, a showcase of liquor worthy of any high-end establishment glittered on illuminated glass shelves. It was garish, but Em prescribed it would've cost more to tear it down and replace with something more reasonable. Besides, garish suited her sometimes. Like her belt.

"My boy!" Em burst at the sight of me.

I smiled wide. "Hey."

I sat in the middle of the long section.

"Your Bellini is on hiatus," Em said. "I sent Austin and Terrence to get ice."

Benny waved his Blue Hawaiian midair to accentuate the lack of clinking.

"Actually," Em said, "I sent *Terrence* to get ice, but you know Austin can't leave his side."

"If they're lucky enough to find ice," Benny said while he scratched his mostly white stubble. "We broke the national record today."

Em said, "Yes, Benny, we've all heard." Then to me: "In the meantime?"

"White wine, I guess."

She turned to the mini fridge.

"On track to break it again tomorrow," Benny went on.

Em retrieved a Riesling and filled a large-bottomed glass to the top. She placed it before my hands on the bar. "And yet, Benny, you continue to risk heat exhaustion in your layered suits."

"Drip before death." Benny cheered no one and drank.

"I don't even know what that means," Em said.

"Style! Fashion!" Benny said in exaggerated offense. When lockdowns forced him to work from home, he became distracted (or enamoured) with the social media apps he'd previously prided himself on avoiding — Twitter, Instagram, and, most notoriously, TikTok. Terrence might've turned him onto it. He and his boyfriend of two years, Austin, had gained what they called *clout* as a couple making cutesy or funny videos during quarantine, but their popularity waned late last year and never recovered. The result: Benny was now fluent in Gen Zed, which did him, as the greyest among us, no favours.

As for Austin, well, we liked Austin, but he wasn't one of the Original Five.

"I prefer swag," Em said. "I am now nostalgic for swag."

"Remember bling?" I said.

"Oh my god, my mom *hated* bling!" Em said.

"I have some saved videos to show you, Collie," Benny said, phone suddenly in hand.

"One glass first," I said. "No Chase?"

"Chase should be on the Malahat right now," Em said.

"Right," I said. "Right."

Chase, the fifth member of our society, needed to visit his mother in Mill Bay. She had been recently released from the hospital after going into diabetic shock (this was as detailed as Chase got)—a condition exacerbated by her refusal to quit drinking. Chase … What else could be said? He was not, perhaps, the sharpest (that would be Em), but he certainly had the sharpest tongue. Tall—almost six-foot-three. Lanky. Poufy hair, too, which I loved to watch during sunsets through Em's tinted window wall, like a wavy bomb, untameable but never messy, never past his ears. And he wore massive aviators everywhere. They covered half his face and made him look like he was smuggling coke circa 1983, but the aesthetic worked for him because he *believed* it worked for him.

And I loved him. I laughed too hard at his jokes. I sputtered too much when he addressed me in casual conversations. I loved him. I'd loved him since he'd bear-hugged me after Michael left.

No Chase tonight, but that was fine. Austin and Terrence would return soon. Still a full house. Not much else to be said about that.

The sound of the door latch downstairs muted us, and soon Terrence appeared, Austin-less, an ice bag in each hand.

"Lords and ladies," he said, "I come with gifts in this desperate hour." Sweat beaded in his dark buzz cut and sopped through his grey muscle shirt.

He placed the bags, wet with condensation, on the counter, and Em stowed them, asked how many places he had to try. Terrence said eight—the Petro-Can on Douglas Street came through. Benny asked where Austin had scurried to. Terrence said home; the exhaustive search had given Austin a headache so he decided to cab home and rest. More likely a small disagreement had escalated to a full public argument, but that remained an unspoken theory.

Em went to work on a fresh round, and soon the four of us clinked glasses of cold cocktails in celebration.

Benny said to Terrence, "I favourited your latest video."

"Thanks, Benny—you're the only one favouriting them these days." Terrence stood beside me at the bar and nudged his side into mine. "And Collie? How's our mole?"

I worked for the Province. An administrative assistant for the Ministry of Environment. Mostly data entry and emails, but it paid my rent and granted me free weekends. It had been a recent coup; beforehand, I'd endured a slew of painstaking retail gigs.

"No plans to abolish gay marriage yet," I said.

"*God!*" Terrence complained. "When will those bureaucrats give me something to whine about?"

Benny said, "Wouldn't that be federal?"

"Shut up, Benny," Terrence said.

Benny ignored him. "Protest fossil fuels."

"Oh, fun," Terrence said.

"Big spill on the Malahat this afternoon," Benny said.

I said, "The Malahat?"

"When?" Em said. "Where?"

"I don't know," Benny said. "I just glanced at the article a few minutes ago and kept scrolling."

Em strode to the end of the bar opposite Benny and reached for the power button to the flatscreen that hung there (another remnant from the previous owner that seemed too much trouble to remove, but it came in handy for *Drag Race* airings). She flicked to the local station, which confirmed it: an aerial shot of a fuel tanker jack-knifed on the mountain pass road just before Goldstream Park. The winding, thin section of highway was blocked on either side by the fallen semi, the tank cracked where it had collided with the cement meridian. Cars were lined up to the edges of the frame in every lane, northbound and southbound. Fuel streamed from the breach in the tanker's hull toward the mountain side of the road. Better than if it were flowing directly into Goldstream River on the other side, grim as that consolation was.

"No timeline for a fix," Benny said, reading from his phone.

Em pointed at the TV. "Look, the cars go all the way to Uptown Mall."

Benny looked up, fascinated. "Jesus. Fender to fender, too."

Terrence snorted obnoxiously enough to trigger Em's own chuckle.

Benny stretched out his arms — *What?*

"*Fender to fender?*" Terrence said. "Bumper to bumper. The fender is over the wheel. Didn't you date a mechanic for five minutes?"

Benny pantomimed a nagging mouth with his hand, then waved Terrence off. "Fender, bumper, whatever. Turn that off. It's Friday. I mean, sucks for everyone involved, but there's nothing we can do. They should've devised an alternative to the Malahat decades ago."

The front door slammed shut, turning our heads to the stairway. Em's music had changed to Britney Spears's 'Toxic'.

"Dear God!" came a voice from the bottom of the stairs. "Dear God!" It was Chase. "Dear God!"

He appeared, soaked in sweat and heaving like the fifteen steps were a taxing workout. He lumbered over to the bar—plain tee, mid-thigh shorts, aviators—and hopped onto the counter, cross-legged. Then he lay back and straightened his legs. His pink socks jabbed my drink, and I snagged it against my chest.

"Chase!" Em said. "God's sake! Off!"

"Minute, Em." Chase dropped one arm behind the bar and blindly reached for the nearby sink's knob. Once his fingers found it, he blasted the cold water and cupped his hand underneath, causing spray in every direction.

"Chase, what the fuck!" Em said. "You're soaking everything, and your hair's greasing up my bar top!"

With his other hand, Chase removed his aviators, suspended them over his head. Then his hand under the tap shot up, slapped his face, and spread coldness into every crevice.

"I walked this whole way," Chase said between dramatic breaths. "This *whole way*. From Uptown Mall."

"You walked here from Uptown?" Benny said.

"You're … a clairvoyant, Benny," Chase huffed. "Actually, I walked to the nearest bus stop and caught the number two, but the closest stop to here is, like, four blocks north."

Em shut the water off and stood over him. "Chase, my patience is here—and you're way over *here*."

Chase's face scrunched in confusion. "You didn't gesture anything."

Em pressed both palms on his hip and pushed.

"Yes, all right, good, *Jesus*, don't push! I'm not a bouncing baby boy anymore." He inelegantly dragged himself off the bar, then pulled his tee back to his waist, hid the black hair around his belly button, and folded his shades and hung them in his collar. He sat two seats away from me.

"Left my car." Chase shrugged in disbelief at Em and then, when she only returned a cocked eyebrow, he pointed to everyone else's drink. "Hard sarsaparilla, my love." Root beer and vanilla vodka—a concoction he alone fancied. "Left it in the parking lot by H&M after I waited *forty-five minutes* in dead traffic. If the buses didn't have their own lanes, I'd be dead myself." Em placed his drink before him, and he bent his head, took a short sip through the metal straw. "Mm! Terrence! Where's your excess weight this evening?"

Terrence pursed his lips. "Headache."

Chase said, "Poor thing. Christ, I was *this* close. I left work at three-fifty this afternoon. What time did that cow on the Malahat tip? Three-twenty-three. *This close.* Had to call Mom. Had to take public transportation. I am distressed."

Em said, "How's your mom?"

"Ugh," Chase said. "Christ, did we not decide on air conditioning for this place? I meant to raise the issue. Collie? How're you?"

I opened my mouth to give some knee-jerk, banal response.

Benny said, "Chase, don't be rude. Em asked about your mom. You just breezed past her."

Chase interlocked his fingers on the counter and leaned forward to better see Benny. "Yes, I did, Benny. I'm sorry, and I'm sorry, Em. I am not myself this afternoon. But perhaps that was my subtle way of suggesting I don't want to talk about it?"

Em said, "All good, dear."

Chase said, "How's *your* mother, Benny? Oh. Right. You don't talk."

"I said *all good*, Chase!" Em said, referee in her own home. "Holster your weapons."

"I apologize." He leaned forward again. "I apologize, Benny. I walked all the way here, you know. I needed so badly to check in on Mom this weekend. Now I'm fraught with paranoia and heatstroke. So I apologize, Benny."

"Fine," Benny said. "We don't all have the luxury of accepting parents."

Em rolled her eyes. "Do I need to put you two in separate corners?"

Terrence said, "Let's move on."

I finished my drink.

"Let's trade, Benny," Chase said. "You get the ill, sixty-six-year-old woman-child who refuses to engage in basic health regimens to keep her out of the hospital and usually reeks like gin when you hug her, like an alcohol-logged sponge, like it comes out of her pores. And I'll lounge in my penthouse, ogling twinks on TikTok."

Terrence excused himself from the bar, drink in hand, and retired to the far corner of the room where two couches bordered a round coffee table.

I swivelled my empty glass. Em caught it and refilled me, her vision now forward and nowhere — invisible blinders to the bitchy queens on either end of her bar. These nights weren't common, but they weren't unusual either. And in this heat? We had been idiots not to call tonight off. Sooner than later, Em would find the end of her patience, and the Two Oh Four Six would be closed like the plethora of queer spaces before it.

"This is where Chase earnestly apologizes again," Benny said.

Chase said, "Honestly, honey, you're thirty-eight years old. Those baby-faced app boys don't love you."

"I am so sick of this subject," Terrence shouted from the corner.

"You can't adjourn to the peanut gallery and then get involved," Chase said.

"Once a week now," Terrence said. "Why do we keep talking like every insufferable boomer we know? It's a platform for creatives, and it has no age restrictions! The end!"

"It's a tool for the Chinese government to determine if you're an enemy of the state," Chase said, "but I know *you* love it because they put you in a higher tax bracket."

Em tore herself from her trance. "It's not on my phone, but I've seen plenty of videos, and these kids get to be who they are at a *much* younger age than we ever did. Could that be why you don't like them, Chase?"

"Don't try to crack this nut, Em," Chase said. "You'll find I'm long expired. And *please*. For every five *hilarious* videos Benny or Terrence foists on us, there's one gay kid or trans teen secretly recording their repulsive excuse for parents screaming at them, promising they are not who they think they are — and if they *try* to be? Said children are cast out. Homeless. Yeah. No shit. Do we have collective amnesia? Some get by earlier than others. Some get by because they're excellent hiders. Sounds like the world I grew up in." He fidgeted with his sunglasses, placed them on the bar. Shaky fingers. Eyes on his root beer vodka. And when the room's silence quaked through us, he added, "The world is cyclical."

"Depends where you live, I guess," Benny said.

Chase hoisted himself off his seat and strolled toward Benny. "You think these kids hold their partners' hands in public and don't feel *entirely* self-conscious?"

"Yes," Terrence piped from the corner.

Chase slung his arm around Benny's shoulders and squeezed. "No. That will never change. We'll never be *normalized*. Lord help me if we come close. What would I do without the attention?"

Terrence was right: at least once a week now, this subject was broached—a subject none of us were equipped to explore correctly, but we macheted through anyway. While workboats gathered to stem the rising tides, while the heat made indoor objects feel oven-baked, while fuel surged loose over roadways, we marched on, braving the only issue we could manage to think about for more than five minutes. A gaggle of half-sober millennials unused to the generation of kids after us getting older, becoming young adults.

"I hope we will be normalized," I said. The room's attention collapsed on me. "I really do. I think I need to trust that we will be."

Now Chase, laser focus on me for the first time this year, approached the seat beside mine. His scent wafted over me—sweat and cologne and dying antiperspirant and vodka. Far too much vodka. It oozed over me, clung to my furrowed eyebrows.

"You're too romantic, Collie." His hand grazed my back.

"Chase, where'd you pre-party?"

"You *would* want to hold hands conscience-free. Or would you just like to hold hands at this point? How many years since Whatshisname split?"

"Michael."

"*Michael.*" The toxins in his breath rushed through my nostrils. "You shouldn't miss him anymore, Collie, but you're too romantic. You'd rather spend the remainder of your provincial life self-consciously holding hands along Dallas Road than never feeling the judgmental gawk of strangers again. What a fucked-up choice. While heteros flaunt it in droves and Studio Ghibli music accompanies them with every footfall."

"Leave Colin alone," Em said.

Chase's eyes pulled on mine — invisible strings. His pupils danced inches from mine like I'd often fantasized. And how fucked up, as he'd put it, that *this* Chase still fulfilled some distant version of those dreams. Anybody else would've tossed his inebriated bones to the floor by now.

Chase pouted. "My poor Collie."

"Did you leave the booze in your car?"

Now those eyes bulged, the oxygen between us densified, and I thought he might hit me — I don't know why, somehow violence defined his face. Instead he was on me faster than the thought could fully metastasize: lips on mine, his plumper but dryer. My eyes darted closed but the rest of me was paralyzed, one hand on my glass and the other straight out like a useless board. Then we parted. It lasted maybe two seconds.

"Left it in the glovie," Chase said.

"You were driving drunk?" Em said, her voice loud and motherly and close.

Chase smirked her way. "Idling drunk, technically."

He came back to me, bottom lip now pressed under his teeth. He slapped my thigh — like a buddy. "You're as hopeless as I am."

He turned his back to me, then shrank as he moved to join Terrence in the corner, where the two of them began discussing an unrelated topic. They spoke at a regular volume, but their voices were murmurs to me. Benny returned to his phone. Em watched me a moment longer, but I couldn't match her eyeline.

This was some new, unspecified sense of shame. When she turned and tended to Benny's near-empty glass, an inexplicable tear pocked my cheek. I struck it off. Was it because I hadn't thought of Michael in over a year, but also hadn't lived a day without him somewhere in my brain? Or because my penchant for romance could only set me up for further cruelty? Neither answer seemed quite right.

My romance was not unlike Chase's need to be the focal point. Not unlike the Two Oh Four Six itself: occupied by half-lived queers—still marginalized but not, still young but not. Every facet of our lives was uncertain, so we needed to invent certainty. Maybe the self-inflicted pageantry we steeped ourselves in was the last method we knew for reminding ourselves that we existed, that we still felt.

Em had already turned off the news. No more. *We're at capacity.*

SHADOW WORK

Soramimi Hanarejima

Soramimi Hanarejima is the author of the neuropunk story collection Literary Devices for Coping, and their recent work can be found in Outlook Springs, Moss, Cotton Xenomorph, and Cheat River Review. Soramimi's story 'The Theft of Confidence' appears in Pulp Literature Issue 17, and 'Practising the Art of Forgetting' appears in Issue 28. 'Shadow Work' was shortlisted for our 2021 Raven Short Story Contest.

Shadow Work

1

After work, we meet in the park near your office and use the late-afternoon sunlight to swap shadows. The instant yours transfers over to me, I recoil at the emotional buildup she's accrued. I expected it to be bad after all these months, but this is ridiculous. Burdened with so much cruft, her mimicry of my movements is perceptibly effortful, still keeping up but always encumbered. My shadow hasn't been this laden with residue since my college years, those times I'd let psychological hygiene fall by the wayside during academically demanding semesters. And much as my studies back then distracted me from the gradual accumulation of affective detritus and its toll, work has kept you from fully appreciating the onus your shadow bears. Until now.

Undoubtedly it's a refreshing change for you to have my shadow — the antithesis of yours, unfettered by the dross of feelings that have run their course. And I, accustomed to always having a well-kempt shadow, become increasingly agitated by the sorry state of your shadow — soon incensed, on the verge of launching into a tirade that shames you for mistreating her.

But the urge to upbraid you quickly subsides. I didn't come here to argue with you. I came here to get this taken care of.

2

By bus, I go to the mountains east of the city. There, I follow the usual trail through the woods and across the valley. Out in the open, the sheen of moonlight on the scrubby expanse creates a mood of desolate beauty, an atmosphere attractive to a painter with philosophical inclinations who would render this scene as 'Landscape with Figure and Shadow'. She, the darkest part of the painting, long and thin on the short, young stalks of grass that seem like they should be getting combed down as she passes over them. Because this silhouette of you feels heavy, and it gets only heavier the farther we go, like I'll soon get tired of towing her across the terrain as she drags across the ground with a viscous inertia that's unsettling—practically the opposite of the way mine glides right over floors, sidewalks, and lawns.

But the weight is of course metaphysical and doesn't slow me down much. I reach the stream near the base of Mt Mindle with plenty of time to carry out the cleansing. At the water's edge, I take off my shoes and socks then step into the cold current and stand on the rocky stream bed in a spot where your shadow can fall fully upon the water's surface. Leaning over her, I reach my hands through your shadow and jostle the water. Barely a moment later, emotional detritus comes off her as a plume of minuscule grit that brushes past my fingers and palms before flowing away, carried off downstream. Yet again, I'm amazed that this age-old practice works so well. What would we do without it? How else would your shadow be relieved of the hefty load you've long saddled her with?

3

On my way back across the valley, your shadow is just the way she should be: light and airy—ethereal, sailing over everything she's cast upon. Until there's a tug at the edges of my shoes, an unmistakable resistance where your shadow connects to me. Probably some stubborn residue I didn't wash out is now hindering her movement.

I stop in my tracks and check my watch. I'm not that far from the stream, but going back means hurrying to catch the last bus. It may be worth it to ensure that your shadow has been thoroughly cleaned. Then there's that pull at my feet again, stronger now—insistent. Looking over at your shadow, I'm surprised to find that she's shaking a pointed index finger vigorously to the right. My gaze follows the direction of her gesture and meets a fire owl perched on the branch of a still-bare tree. Moonlight has made its feathers into the orange flames of its namesake, like a little inferno that could ignite the dark mesh of the forest behind it into a conflagration. I marvel at the radiant bird of prey then continue on. Further down the trail, another tug at my shoes brings my attention to your shadow—who is again pointing emphatically, this time to an opalescent moonbow over a waterfall in the distance.

She does this all along the length of the trail, alerting me to interesting things in the nocturnal landscape, little nuggets of delight that punctuate the return trek to the bus stop—among them, Zintewofs swinging through the high branches of the forest canopy and fern maples leafing out, each tiny bit of new foliage still curled and wrinkled, in the middle of an imperceptibly slow emergence from the bud it was tightly cocooned within all winter. You've never mentioned anything about your shadow behaving this way. Maybe she's presenting me with these sights in exchange for the cleansing, or maybe she's reinvigorated and enthusiastic about the world again.

When I board the bus back to the city, I take one of the tandem seats so the interior lighting places her on the seat beside me. There's nothing noteworthy here for her to point out, but I want to remain aware of her as we are ferried through the darkness back to the city.

4

In the morning, I remember that I have your shadow only after sunrise, when the orange light streaming through the window casts her on the floor tiles while I'm at the kitchen counter. The elongated silhouette moves with fluid ease as I put water and ground coffee into the coffeemaker.

When I take a few sips of coffee during breakfast, her hands flutter across the kitchen table. She must be enlivened by the caffeine thrum that passes from me through her into the table. This is probably new to her. You don't drink coffee.

5

When I arrive at the park, you're already waiting for me on one of the benches shaded by oak trees, out of the abundant springtime sunshine that will make swapping back easy. Seeing me approach, you rise swiftly and walk over, my shadow emerging from those of the trees.

On the recently mowed grass, we stand barefoot, back to back like children comparing their heights after a growth spurt. The backs of our heels touch, and my shadow snaps to my feet with a jolt of warmth. And … that's it. Your shadow stays attached to me, even after we wait a couple minutes.

"Looks like she doesn't want to go back," I say.

"I don't blame her," you reply. "But she's mine. She has to come back."

"She probably just needs some time."

"Yeah, some more time away from me and my psychologically slovenly lifestyle."

And why would she ever go back to that? What are you offering her that's worth returning to?

These irritation-sparked sentiments blaze in my mind, and I want to fling them at you, but the impulse to berate you quickly wanes.

"Well, why don't we try again later in the week, then," I suggest instead.

And we leave it at that.

6

It takes me much of the day to get the hang of having two shadows, to figure out how to move through life with a new psychological center of gravity—like I'm a cat learning poise and a new gait after suddenly gaining a second tail that moves independently of the tail I've always known. The shadows dissipate different emotions at different rates—mine diffusing everything gradually, yours almost exclusively dispersing the negative with incredible celerity.

This reminds me of the last time I had two shadows. Decades ago, I had Mom's in addition to my own, both of them doing the emotional work only shadows can, mine by instinct, hers with a discernment honed by years of experience — providing examples to develop my shadow's intuition. Sometimes, I felt like I had only one shadow. Mine would let Mom's take the lead and hide in her, especially if we were in a crowded place buzzing with energy.

By late afternoon, I've mostly adjusted to the new arrangement. Still, something seems … off. Jocular conversations with colleagues lose their flair within minutes, turning sedate. When I get back to work on some breakup memories for one of my usual clients, the sting of the relationship's end is no longer as sharp. These and other odd little occurrences tell me that I've got some way to go before I'm accustomed to having two shadows.

7

After work, I forgo today's happy-hour outing with friends and head straight home, fatigued by all the recalibrating of my metaphysical balance. I just want to have a mug of tea on the veranda, and, once I'm home, I do exactly that. As I stand outside, staring at the cityscape of concrete and glass, the cool air and grassy warmth of the sencha lull me into a trance. The shallow angle of the sun stretches both shadows off to my right, across almost the entire length of the veranda, making me a sundial with two long hands close together.

When I come back inside, I head to the kitchen to make dinner. My plans are abruptly interrupted when the big toe of my right foot strikes something hard, sending a jolt of pain through me. Once the shock ebbs and I'm able to think again, I realize that my toe collided against the partially assembled meaning synthesizer on the living room floor. With my mug still in hand (thankfully), I hobble over to the sofa, upset that I've allowed this unfinished personal project to be a tripping hazard. But a moment later—when I've just sunk into the sofa's velvet cushions—I'm no longer annoyed at myself, despite my injured toe throbbing at full force.

"You have to let me feel it," I tell your shadow, even though that fervent heat of exasperation has already gone cold.

When the pain has dulled to an ache, an idea forms in my mind—an explanation for your shadow's psychological debris: she's relieving you of intense negative emotions too quickly. With your reactive temperament, this would naively seem the right thing to do. Better, presumably, for you to burn briefly with a flash of anger than to simmer with indignation. But it's the simmering that can lead to reflection. Denied time to run their course, emotions will lack depth and nuance. And that favours the rise of more emotions, ones that she will likely also curtail, continuing the cycle. More emotions in you means more residue on your shadow.

Though only a hunch, this explanation has a plausibility which compels me to convince your shadow to dispel emotions with a deliberate slowness. But how? Maybe I could intentionally make myself jealous or frustrated, then hold on to the emotion, refusing to relinquish it to her until my psyche has been fully jostled by its fervour. Or is it more effective to carry out some regimen of emotional exercises? I'll stop by the library tomorrow after work and ask for books on shadow training.

8

Thursday morning in the memory studio is quiet — just me extrapolating what vividness I can from a client's transient impressions — until you call. I've barely answered the phone when you frantically insist that we meet immediately. In a flurry of taut words, you tell me that a check-in with management has riled you up and you've been roiling with exasperation ever since. Venting to co-workers and performing deep-breathing exercises have proven ineffective against this emotional churn.

Encounters with management often agitate you, but never have you called me with such panicked urgency during the workday. So I take my lunch break early and head over to the academic district.

9

Back in the park, we stand on the sun-drenched grass with the rears of our heels pressed together, sandwiching between them the leather of your shoes and the canvas of mine. We really should do this barefoot, but you're in a desperate hurry. Your shadow, though, isn't in any hurry, still reluctant to return to you. After some hesitation, she relents and slowly rejoins you, probably unable to leave you unaided in this time of need. You heave a sigh of audible — palpable — relief.

Once we're facing each other again, you're considerably calmer, your expression now the epitome of blissful ease.

No, I want to say to her, *not so quickly. Time is the key to unlocking change through learning.*

"Oh, *man*," you murmur. "Thank you *so much*. Everything feels way better now."

After a moment, you add, "I'm going to practise better psychological hygiene from now on. Avoid situations that trigger me. Watch for when I'm spiralling into emotional drama so I can stop myself. And, of course, shadowbathe *every month*."

That final part of your vow prompts my gaze to flit over to your shadow. She seems to be giving me a thumbs-up. And though the apparent gesture could simply be a result of the sunlight hitting your hands, I take it as an indication that her reluctance to return to you was a bid to get you to practise better self-care. At some point, you're now likely to make a bid to get me to go out with you on a night with a full moon and clear skies.

My heart races as my chest tightens, and my mind is composing a preemptive rebuff, but a few seconds later, all that agitation unwinds, and in my peripheral vision, my shadow is shaking her head, the rhythmic movement soothing — reassuring.

Right, let's simply take things as they come. Whatever future with you lies ahead, I'll inhabit it once it becomes our present.

THE ISLAND

M Denise Beaton

M Denise Beaton *lives in Vancouver with her partner and their puppy. She is a PhD student in Population and Public Health and has an MA in Gerontology. She works in public policy and writes short stories on her lunch break. She has authored or co-authored five academic manuscripts, but this is her first published work of fiction. All her life, she has dreamed of a reader like you.*

The Island

The Tourism Board decided to create an island only for women. That is not to say they built it; rather, one of the 102 islands off the coast was designated for the project. Someone reading the news may note the curious lack of women on the Tourism Board. The idea sprang like Athena from the heads of men. It is easier to create an oasis — or ghetto, depending on who you ask — than to work towards a society from which half the population does not need a vacation.

I was among the flood of applicants for a job at the new hotel.

"You're a rat in the Tourism Board's experiment," my sister said.

Maybe. But I was well-paid, and awareness of an experiment does not make a rat.

The first few months as a concierge at the Wellspring Hotel flew by. As far as I know, the menstrual cycles of the women on the Island did not sync up, contrary to the fears of the Tourism Board. Like all new businesses, the initial influx of interest raised hopes. But of course, it wasn't an insular sisterhood. There was stratification: the women who worked, and the women who didn't.

The women bathed in the shallows, sang sweetly, and combed one another's long hair. At least they did in the minds of the men who frequented the other 101 islands, and who set out in boats to catch a glimpse. A joke among the media, but a reminder to women that the only true freedom was in our minds.

The Island was two hours by boat from the mainland. The *Krystyna*, a tired ferry with a fresh coat of paint and a fresh name, had rosé smashed over her hull and began the business of carting passengers. It wasn't a new boat, but then again, it wasn't a new island.

The hotel workers, the groundskeepers, and the outdoor activity coordinators slept in bungalows—or barracks, depending on who you ask—located a fifteen-minute walk into the woods. It was the perfect solution to obscure workers from the view of guests and to sate the hunger of insects living in the thick pine brush.

The trail was cut to accommodate single-file passage, an unnecessary measure to prevent lingering fraternization.

The trail ended in a clearing next to the parked golf carts for activity coordinators. The Wellspring Hotel crouched atop the gentle swell of a hill, giving way on the other side to a pebbled beach that functioned as an unauthorized souvenir shop. On the left were tennis courts, and to the right were the docks, ferry pier, and heated pool. Of course, no one could swim in the ocean anymore, but the lengths of the pool were level with the Atlantic and the hotel marketed its chlorinated waters as the next best thing.

The sunrise stretched bands of pink and yellow across the sky, and I pulled my pant legs loose from my socks. Humidity accumulated over the day, often bringing thunderstorms at night. At dawn the air was cool and clear. I preferred to walk to the hotel alone, away from the crush of other women. Each small cabin slept eight and was so close to the next that an outstretched arm through the window grazed fingertips against shingled wood. At the hotel, my face spent eight hours smiling. Each morning the manager, Mrs Winchester, gathered the concierge staff in a huddled circle and exclaimed that we were the first and last impression of Wellspring. We softened our faces like pliant wax to better bear the brand.

Through the wonder of uniforms, the concierge staff appeared interchangeable: young, average in both height and weight, pleasantly pretty yet not challengingly beautiful, hair plaited, nails filed, no jewellery.

We welcomed guests and bid them goodbye, suggested activities, and passed along messages. The lack of wireless internet and cellular reception was twisted into a selling point, but not everyone wanted to unplug. The concierge computers had a hardwired internet connection, as did the computers in the back offices. While it was outside our original job description, we often checked personal email for guests, reading aloud or turning our screens towards them and our eyes away. At first, I was surprised how little they cared what we saw: bank statements, love letters, dispatches from work, feuds with family. I quickly realized concierge staff were another amenity, like the complimentary Wellspring stationery. Blank and unlined.

We ate our meals in shifts in the staff dining room. On our weekly day off, we were permitted to wander the Island or take the ferry to the mainland. We wore cornflower polo shirts and beige chinos when working, and raspberry polo shirts when off duty. At no time were we to be mistaken for guests.

The hotel was on the south side, with the meadow and the deep green forest stretching northwards, made inviting by distance. Other than the narrow swath cut through the brush and the clearing for the staff cabins, the forest was impenetrable. If you headed east along the perimeter, however, forty minutes' worth of walking granted access to a white-sand beach and dunes choked with wild rose bushes. I spent my days off there, with a book and some scraps smuggled from the kitchen. Mrs Winchester feared mice, and workers were forbidden to eat outside of the staff dining room. I wrapped food in a napkin and tucked it in my chinos for later, gleaning sustenance as much from the mild rebellion as from what was crumpled in my pockets. My cabin mates teased me that I fasted on my off-days, went on pilgrimages, sought enlightenment. They probably sensed the truth that I was avoiding them.

At the hotel, I existed solely in the present, turning towards the needs of guests like a sunflower following the brightest star. The workers lived their off-hours in the future, talking about what they were saving for. Many were taking a gap year before college, or planning to work for six months and spend the rest of the year travelling. Some were saving for their weddings, others simply waiting to age into their trust funds. I was not enrolled in college or university, no wedding was planned, my family offered neither trust nor funds, and I could not imagine myself in a foreign country. Thoughts of the future felt like descending stairs and missing a step. The only clear thing was that I did not want to model my life after anyone I knew, and this job was the cotyledon of my independence.

I ignored the rain until a heavy drop splattered against my page. I tucked my book under my shirt, hunched against the sting of rain now falling quickly, and walked down the beach to take shelter under a rocky outcropping. I watched the sand darken and pellets of rain disappear into the surf. The waves met at a dark-blue streak rippling the surface of the water. My grandmother, who swam in the ocean as a child, told me about rip currents. *Calm water in choppy waves looks the safest but is the most dangerous.*

My only childhood swimming had taken place in the weekly bath, soap scum from my mother and sister floating like seafoam. I made waves with my hands in the cooled water, swirling the washcloth and its maroon-tinged cork passengers in the tempest. My mother rolled her eyes when my grandmother taught me things I didn't need to know, but children don't weigh the worth of stories on scales of practicality. I loved hearing how to survive what I would not experience. Walking along the beach I recited what I remembered: *Stay calm. You cannot outswim. Conserve energy. You will need it. It moves in a circle. Let it bring you back.*

Soon the cloud passed and the murky beach smelled rich and earthy. A jolt of colour winked in the deep current of water. Neon orange. I watched it bob until it was carried beyond my vision. The soft blur of natural colours over the last two months at the Wellspring had lulled me.

Whatever was ferried by the rip current would be deposited farther down the beach. I followed the curve of the Island north, soft dunes yielding to forest thick with the hum of insects. Neon orange. Drawing closer, I realized it was a large sneaker. I picked it up, startled by its weight, and a foot slid out, hitting the sand with a soft thud.

I don't remember how I got back to the cabin. I bagged my dirty clothes, showered, and changed into my second set. I walked the trail to the Wellspring stiffly, fighting the urge to run. After an apologetic visit with the laundry room attendant, I knocked on Mrs Winchester's office door.

"Come in," Mrs Winchester called.

Her office was as large as one of our cabins.

"Yes? I'm very busy, what do you want?"

"I found a foot."

"A foot." Mrs Winchester closed her laptop and swivelled to face me.

"In a sneaker, on the beach, on the north side of the Island."

"Sit down. Did you tell anyone about this foot?"

"No."

"Good girl. See that you don't." She twirled her pen rapidly between four fingers like a small baton. "It would cause unnecessary concern."

I nodded.

"A lot of people want to see us fail. I've watched you work the front desk, you know. You're obviously not as thrilled with customer service as the other girls." She smiled, red lipstick on incisors. "But then again, what animal doesn't chafe at a yoke? Perhaps you would prefer some solitary work walking on the beach, as you seem to like to do."

I twisted my fingers in my lap.

"Of course, the alternative is to quit. Or be fired. I've had some complaints about you. From the guests and the girls. And you signed a lengthy contract — probably didn't read through it, did you, about the defamation and breach of confidentiality clauses, hm? Just in case you want to cause a little stir on the mainland."

Sweat bloomed under my arms.

"No, you're smarter than that." Mrs Winchester held her pen aloft, cleared her throat. "Ankles are weak, and a foot separates easily from a body submerged in the water." She bobbed the pen between her fingers. "Sneakers are buoyant, perfect vessels to carry foul messages to shore. This island is within crossing tides, you see, and any accidents or suicides, well."

She placed the pen on her desk.

"We can't have guests finding out that men have been setting foot, as it were, on the Island. How about I relieve you from your desk duties and entrust you with patrolling the shoreline? Anything you find, take a photo of it for me and then bury it. The soil keeps secrets better than the sea."

She watched me closely. My mouth was dry.

"Of course, with a change in responsibilities, you would be moved into the hotel. A room to yourself, comfort, access to facilities. Anyone would kill for that kind of upgrade. So, tell me, can you keep a secret? Are you like the soil, or are you like the sea?"

Stay calm. You cannot outswim.

My things were moved to the hotel that afternoon. Mrs Winchester sent a small shovel and a slice of cake to my room. *Congratulations!* exclaimed the chocolate sauce on the plate.

Each day I walked the perimeter of the Island. It took six hours. *Conserve energy. You will need it.*

In the months that followed, I found and buried eight feet. At night I dreamed of them sprouting.

It moves in a circle. Let it bring you back.

In the fall, I told Mrs Winchester I was going to see my family. If she realized it was my first time visiting the mainland, she did not question. That morning I left my belongings in my room, my shovel tucked in the bed.

My bank account was full enough now to provide choice.

From the stern of the *Krystyna*, I watched eight brightly coloured objects, washed clean of soil, bob against the pebbled beach.

5 WAYS OF SHUTTING UP

Dawn Macdonald

Dawn Macdonald lives in Whitehorse, Yukon, where she was raised off the grid. She holds a degree in applied mathematics and used to know a lot about infinite series. Her poetry has recently appeared or is forthcoming in Asimov's Science Fiction, The Malahat Review, *and* Strange Horizons.

5 Ways of Shutting Up

1.

Do you like our sexual dimorphism, I ask.
He likes the way I fit into his armpit.
Inside the pit of the peach is a soft thing, and bitter.
A tongue out of the mouth.

2.

Loose lips sink ships.
Sunk ships drip drops.
Dropped drips plink plonk.
Plonked plinks clog sinks.

3.

Deep morning is a velvet box
and I a dull jewel, snug within.
The lid is prised up from the horizon.
Some hand will wear this ring.

4.
Like a telescope.
Like a lawn chair.
Like a freezerdoor.
Like a coffintop.
Like a conibear.

5.
Gulped down a gumball
from the 25¢ machine.
Kids say if you eat one it'll
swell in your guts and kill you.
You're gonna die
kid.

FLOATERS

Kevin Sandefur

Kevin Sandefur *is the capital projects accountant for the Champaign Unit 4 School District. His stories have recently appeared in* The Saturday Evening Post, The Gateway Review, The Sunlight Press, *and* Bethlehem Writers Roundtable. *His story 'Out in the Sticks' won an honourable mention in our 2021 Hummingbird Flash Fiction Prize contest and appears in Issue 33. And 'Floaters' received an honourable mention in our 2021 Raven Short Story Contest. Kevin lives with his wife and two cats in Champaign County, Illinois, which is a magical place where miracles happen almost every day and hardly anyone seems to find that remarkable.*

*F*LOATERS

If you're asking me did I know Zeke Fido, I'd have to say no, not really, except of course in the biblical sense, but that's probably not what you meant. The reporters all called him 'The Man Who Believed He Could Fly', which was the title of that special they did on him, but I wasn't in it much, which is just fine by me, if anybody's asking. Which I guess you kind of are.

You may not believe this, since hardly anybody mentions him much anymore, but for a while there, they couldn't talk about anything else. I met Zeke during the year of the floaters, which is obviously where he got the idea. The Institute had dedicated the first ward to them, and Zeke and I both worked there as night-shift nurses. He was good at his job, always there to help before you called, always efficient and professional. I appreciated that, but mostly I just thought he was drop-dead gorgeous.

I couldn't take my eyes off him as we moved from bed to bed, loosening each patient's restraints so they could drift up to eye level for the doctors' morning rounds. He clearly cared deeply about all of our patients. You could tell by the way he moved around them, gently easing them upwards so they wouldn't jerk at the end of their straps.

When we'd get to the end of the room, we would wait together, standing by in case the doctors needed anything. They shepherded their interns through the ward, pretending to examine each patient. You know how they are, peering under the floating bodies like they might discover for the first time what nobody else had seen yet, namely what was holding these people up in the middle of the air. You already know they never did figure it out, not after all the tissue samples and blood draws and image scans and what simple tests they were allowed to run on the living.

After a while they gave up. They never had all that much to go on anyway, just a bunch of patients in comas who no longer felt compelled to obey gravity. My theory was that it was supposed to be the Rapture but heaven was full, so the rest had to stay here. Zeke called my idea the Napture.

His own theory was more elegant. He thought they were all dreaming they were flying, and that gave them the faith they needed to float. When I asked him how that was possible, he said it wasn't, but there they were anyway, proof positive once and for all that people could fly. And there we were, still taking care of them, long after the interns stopped coming and the doctors made fewer and fewer visits, and the news cycles moved on to the next big thing, and the public lost interest.

For a while the bodies just kept coming, and I wondered if we'd have to open another ward, since we only had fifty beds on the top floor. But they stopped once we got to forty-seven. We never did fill those last few beds. Zeke and I would use them for catnaps or to update charts. Sometimes, in the middle of the night, we'd use them for other things. Neither of us made that much noise, and besides, the floaters never seemed to mind.

On those nights, when it was just the two of us, Zeke would go around and loosen all their restraints again to let the patients rise up a few feet. He said it was to prevent bed sores, but I think he really just liked the idea of them hovering, the marvel of it. When they were up off their beds like that, they bobbed up and down in our wake whenever we walked past, surfing an invisible ocean.

Sometimes Zeke would open a window to air out the ward, and if there was a breeze, the patients would wave back and forth like a field of flowers. Zeke called them 'wave people', which he thought was more respectful than just 'floaters'. He felt a real bond with them, and after a while, so did I. I envied their calm, and their peace, their faces all relaxed with that expression morticians always try for but never quite get.

We drifted through most of the summer that way, lost in our own private garden of flotsam and dreams, until the night one of the doctors came back at the start of our shift and told us that the ward was being closed and the patients transferred to a new research facility for long-term study, and that we should get them all ready to move in the morning.

Zeke didn't take that well at all. He stewed about it most of the night. He hated the idea of our patients, *our* patients, being locked in the basement of some government lab, strapped down while somebody opened them up and took them apart and poked around inside, maybe even while they were still alive, hearts pumping away, lungs breathing stale, antiseptic air. I asked him what we could do, but I guess I already knew the answer, because he didn't say anything, just stared at me and hypnotized me with that smile, that beautiful, beautiful smile that said *let's do this, you know you want to.*

The next thing I remember, we were loosening the straps on the patients, unplugging their IVs and monitors and catheters, moving as quickly as we could from one to the next, freeing them from the bonds of medical society. They drifted slowly to the ceiling, straps hanging loose from their sides, until the room was full of floating bodies.

Zeke opened the French doors at the end of the ward and we stepped out onto the small balcony. The sky was already getting lighter in the east. I peeked over the railing and spotted the ground floor doorway some fifty feet directly below us, where I knew there would be security guards. At least they weren't outside.

Zeke and I looked at each other one last time as if to ask whether we were sure. So much for our med careers. We drew the patients, one at a time, slowly by their straps to the opening, pulling them down slightly so they could bob through the door frame like bouquets of get-well balloons, and then out to the balcony.

Once we released them, each patient rose into the night sky, lit from below only by the lights in the parking lot. Above the level of the roof, the morning breeze pushed them slowly toward the dawn. We had three or four of them on their way before the guards on the first floor could see them through the doors. I heard the guards come outside and shout up at us, so I knew we didn't have much time.

Zeke locked the doors to the ward, but they opened outward, so there really wasn't any way to barricade them. We started grabbing patients two or three at a time and queuing them up in the centre of the room like our own little Macy's parade, then took turns running with each one down the length of the aisle and launching them from the balcony.

The pounding on the doors kept getting louder, and we kept moving faster, until we grabbed the last patient and sprinted together through the French doors, catching ourselves on the railing and knocking a flower pot over the edge as we flung our last charge skyward.

The clay pot exploded on the pavement below, just missing a guard and making a perfect star of debris and flowers and shards. The floaters drifted higher and higher into the morning clouds, glowing softly on their way toward the sunrise. Zeke asked me where I thought they would go, but I didn't have any idea. Up, I guessed.

The ward doors sounded like they were coming apart when Zeke turned to me and said the thing I probably knew was coming. We should go with them, he said. I wondered how. He said we could do it the same way as the floaters. We just needed to believe.

I told him I was sorry, but I didn't think I could. That's when the doors at the other end of the ward finally burst open and the security guards came pouring through. Zeke looked at me and nodded, and then he smiled — one last, breathtaking, all-encompassing Zeke smile. He kissed me on the forehead and, with a wink, vaulted over the railing. You know the rest.

AUDREY AND THE CROW

Cadence Mandybura

Cadence Mandybura's fiction has been published in FreeFall, NōD, Fudoki Magazine, and the Bacopa Literary Review. She is a graduate of the Writer's Studio at Simon Fraser University, the associate producer of The Truth podcast, a freelance editor, and a taiko drummer. Cadence's first appearance in Pulp Literature was in Issue 29, with two stories that claimed the top spots for our 2020 Hummingbird Flash Fiction Prize. 'Audrey and the Crow' won an honourable mention in our 2021 Raven Short Story Contest. Learn more at cadencemandybura.com.

AUDREY AND THE CROW

Audrey was seven when she met the crow. (Seven: four fingers on one hand, three on the other, easier than trying to say it aloud.) Play was sweeter now that school was out, and Audrey spent her first morning of freedom in the half-wild acre behind her home, despite the gravelly clouds.

Last summer, Audrey had shared almost every day with Janey, her best friend since preschool. The long highway drives between their homes were easily forgotten, dissolved by morning expeditions, afternoon crafts, and campfire sleepovers. But Janey hadn't been playing with Audrey lately, drifting instead to the girls who snickered whenever Audrey couldn't get her words out in class.

So this year, Audrey was alone when the sky tipped and the world drummed with rain. Closer to the trees than her house, Audrey ducked under a curtain of leaves into her willow cave, scrunching close to the trunk to stay dry. She rubbed her arms and listened. No grumbles yet, just fresh washes of rainfall smacking leaves and dirt. If it thundered, she would have to go back inside.

A rustle to her left: a crow, also escaping the rain, eyed her with a flickering intelligence. Rain braided down the willow's drooping branches, doming Audrey and the crow in the smell of leaves and damp earth.

Not wanting to startle the bird, Audrey slowly twisted the hem of her skirt. The water bunched and ran down her hands, clinging to her homemade bracelets. The crow sprayed his feathers into a ruff with a few brisk shakes. Audrey giggled.

"Caw," said the crow, his feathers settling back into ribbon-smooth lines.

"Caw," Audrey repeated instinctively, then grinned wide because the sound had come out so easily. She was used to words tangling in her mouth, leaving her stuck in the agony between her thoughts and her speech.

The crow cocked his head—then started as a sneaky drop of rain splashed on his back.

"Caw!" he said, but a little different this time—surprised, cross. He ruffled his feathers more brusquely.

Audrey tried this second caw, too, shaking herself until her hair bounced against her forehead. Then she stilled, and waited.

He tipped his head the other way. Hopped closer. A few more balls of water thudded into their sanctuary.

The crow spoke again: not a caw this time, but a warble—slow-rolling syllables with a curl of humour. He seemed to expect a response, so Audrey pulled her ears forward and made a face, then made the funny sound herself.

He jumped sideways, one-footed, and bobbed his head. Audrey laughed and tried the word again. They traded the warble-word back and forth, like a game of catch; her throws got better each time. Eventually, he made a new sound, a rhythmic *ah-ah-ah* in a high, sweet bird voice.

"Oh, b-b-birdie," said Audrey. "My laugh suits you!"

"I've made a friend," Audrey told her parents at dinner, swinging her legs under her chair.

"What's her name?" asked her dad, forking more salad onto Audrey's plate.

"I think it's a b-b-boy," she said. Although she wasn't sure. He just seemed like a boy to her.

Her dad glanced at her mom, who shrugged.

"And his name is …" Audrey had practised all afternoon to get it right: a long, low sound, almost a hum. (The crow had *ah-ah-ah*ed merrily at her first human-tongued attempts.) She took a deep breath and repeated the name for her parents.

Her mom's eyes went wide; her dad laughed. "That's an … unusual name," he said. "Is he not from around here?"

"He's a crow."

"*Oh*," said her mom, her shoulders relaxing. "Can you say his name in English for us?"

"Ummm …" Audrey hadn't even thought to translate his name. In her head it was just in Crow. She said the name to herself again. It reminded her a bit of the steady thrum of rain on leaves. "Maybe … S-S-Storm?"

Her dad turned his mouth down and nodded in appreciation, the same way he did when one of his favourite songs came on. "Crows are very smart," he said. "He should make a good friend."

"You don't want to invite Janey over sometime?" said her mom. "I bet she'd love Storm."

Audrey shrugged and pushed her salad around her plate. If she hid the celery horseshoes under some lettuce, she might get away with not eating them.

"Okay," said her mom, reaching over to rub Audrey's shoulder. "Eat up. You've got your session with Soledad tonight."

"Ugh." She had forgotten that her speech sessions didn't stop with the school year.

"Don't *ugh* Soledad. She's there to help you."

"I know." *There* meant on the other side of a computer screen. Soledad lived far away, a big city somewhere.

"And hopefully the internet won't act up again tonight."

"Mm-hmm."

"Oh, babe, that reminds me — I saw another listing in the city today ..."

Audrey tuned out the conversation as it shifted to a boring parent level. She wondered what words Storm would teach her tomorrow.

Audrey met Storm every day that summer, learning a little more each time. She didn't bother speaking to him with the human words that gave her so much trouble, happy instead to caw, croak, croon, and coo through Crow vocabulary. He clicked in satisfaction as she learned new words, like once when Audrey spied the red scurry of a millipede and said the Crow word for 'bug'.

Storm was clever, watchful, and playful. He paid attention to other living things and their patterns, from crawlies underfoot to lichen spackling the trees to hawks floating high above. As for humans, some were perfectly safe, Storm told Audrey, and some were not. The important thing was that you never knew, at first, what type of human it was. The dangerous ones you had to divebomb.

He demonstrated, targeting one of Audrey's dolls in smooth, scooping attacks.

"Enemy! Enemy! Enemy!" he shrieked.

Audrey mimicked the harsh cry, enjoying its full-throated aggression. It was the best outdoor voice she could imagine. "Enemy! Enemy! Enemy!"

As they yelled, Audrey heard other Crow voices clatter to life, multiplying the warning. She clapped a hand over her mouth to keep her laugh in. Storm was going to be in *so* much trouble.

Sure enough, a dozen members of Crow's family showed up, one of them even clipping Audrey above her ear as it landed. Storm chattered an explanation to them. Although Audrey's Crow wasn't strong enough to follow the conversation, she could tell that Storm's family was giving him heck for his false alarm. Eventually, the cawing calmed, and they turned their shiny eyes towards Audrey. Storm wavered from side to side.

Audrey rubbed her head in the uneasy silence. This felt a bit like the class presentation she'd done about Mercury—or tried to do. She hadn't been able to get past the word *planet* and had broken down in tears.

She cleared her throat, curled her tongue back, and tested the roof of her mouth.

In Crow, she said, "Friend?"

The birds rippled their feathers, muttered to each other. Audrey didn't catch the words, but she noticed Storm bob a little taller.

"Friend," she repeated. "Storm and me—friends."

Two of the crows huffed and flew away. Another one hesitated, cawed weakly, then followed. But the rest stayed to chat, and Audrey got to meet some of Storm's family. He hopped to her side and nuzzled her knee, helping her with everyone's names.

Later, when Audrey went back to the house for lunch, her mom asked where her doll was.

"The willow," said Audrey, but her mom looked confused. "For Storm to play with. What?"

"I asked where you left your doll."

"Oh," said Audrey, realizing that she had spoken in Crow. "The w-w-willow."

By August, Audrey and Storm were carrying on full conversations — although it was the best type of friendship, one that didn't need a lot of words. Audrey brought him nibbles and puzzles, knots to untie, anything shiny. She often lugged her craft kit outside, threading and knotting bracelets as Storm delighted in the multicoloured beads.

Audrey still had weekly speech sessions, and to please her parents, she did her exercises every day. But she didn't care anymore about getting past the wall in her mouth when she tried to speak human words. Learning Crow was hard, but with Storm, at least she didn't feel broken. And without school, Janey and the mean girls seemed a million miles away.

But just when Audrey was happiest came the family meeting. The impossible news.

A new home. New school. New friends. A new Soledad. And no Storm.

No matter how softly her parents spoke, the words cut like glass.

Audrey hadn't thrown a tantrum for years, and her dad had to pin her arms when she started throwing her toys. She yelled until she cried, her throat scraped bloody. "Enemy! Enemy! Enemy!"

When she exhausted her voice, her dad's grip turned into a hug, and he hummed to her like he had when she was younger. She felt her mother's hand, gentle and cool, alight on her head.

"It's okay, baby," said her mom. "You'll see that it's for the best." Her pitch changed, directed at Audrey's dad. "Not a moment too soon."

The next day, Audrey refused to speak to her parents and went straight to the willow cave after breakfast. Storm was his usual self. She set a bowl of cashews between them and watched him eat happily—his knobbled dinosaur feet, his feathers full of subtle shades, his beak so precise and intelligent.

He finished the cashews and looked up at her.

"That's all I brought," she said, opening her palms.

Storm flitted over to a limb overhanging the blackberry bush that hugged the fence. He cawed a question at her.

Audrey's voice caught. She hadn't wanted to tell him. Out here, she could pretend that summer lasted forever, that her parents' plans weren't real, that the idea of boxing up their home and moving to a city was just a bad fairy tale.

Instead of answering, she stood up, stepped out of the willow cave, and started picking blackberries. Storm grabbed a fruit and gobbled it quickly. Too smart to be deterred, he blinked at her and repeated his question.

Audrey ate a berry but knew she couldn't stall forever. Doing her best with her Crow words—*gone, sad, soon*—she told Storm the truth.

He didn't say anything right away. He tugged at her sleeve with his beak, reminding Audrey of a boy in her class who scuffed his shoe against the ground when he didn't know what to say. Then Storm stole another berry.

She thought he might say *sad*, or maybe *stay*, but when he spoke, all he said was, "Friend here now."

"But I will be leaving," Audrey said. "I'll miss you." She wasn't sure she'd got it right, though. Verb tenses were tricky in Crow.

"Better berry patch over here," said Storm, and he hopped away to show her.

Audrey thought about Storm as she tried to sleep that night. He didn't seem upset the same way she was, but maybe that wasn't surprising. As long as he had something to eat or play with, not much seemed to bother Storm. Every day was exciting to him. He didn't have to worry about a new school, making friends, or weekly therapy sessions.

Maybe it was because crows didn't think much about the future, at least not until it butted right into today. He *would* be sad when she left, she was sure; he just didn't realize it yet. But by then it would be too late.

The day before the move, Audrey brought a shoebox to the willow cave and cawed a hello. Storm showed up right away, preening his feathers cheerfully, like always.

Audrey held out the shoebox. "In," she said with a smile.

Without hesitation, Storm flew into the box and set about searching the corners for a treat.

Audrey closed the lid and started tying it shut with old shoelaces.

"Empty," complained Storm.

"I'll feed you on the trip," said Audrey.

His beak poked out of the holes, testing one after the other. "No game," he said. Audrey's heart twinged. She should have left him a toy, even just a ball of twine to pull apart.

"Audrey and Storm stay together!" she said, picking up the box and walking back to the house. "Long trip!"

His claws scrabbled at the holes. "No game," he repeated. "Out!"

"It's just for a short time," Audrey said, trying to find the right words for her plan: quiet, secret, car, new home. Friends forever.

"Out!" Storm shouted. "Out, out, out, out, out!" Audrey's hands grew damp and hot. She gripped the box tighter and tried some of the soothing warbles she had learned from Storm.

He fell silent for a moment. Thinking this was a good sign, she continued her shaky crooning. It would all be okay. It would all be okay …

In the loudest voice she had ever heard Storm use, he raised the alarm. "Enemy! Enemy! Enemy! Enemy! Enemy! Enemy! Enemy!"

"Shh!" she said, rattling the box. She tried to say something else, but found she was gulping with tears. "*Ouch!*" Something had hit the back of her head. Another shriek joined Storm's. *Bam*: another impact, jostling Audrey a step forward. She dropped the box and raised her hands to protect her head. The air was suddenly full of crows and Crow words marking her as a danger. Two of Storm's friends had already landed on the box and were pulling her shoelace fastenings apart.

Audrey ran.

Her parents didn't know why she was so upset. They held her and wiped her face, murmuring comfort, but couldn't understand her words when she tried to explain what had happened.

They made her a cup of cocoa and got her into bed early. Read her favourite story and brought out her old blankie. They said they knew it was scary to move, but they loved her very much and their family would make it through all the changes together. Audrey turned her face to the wall, babbling Crow words without thinking. *Sad. Friend gone. Enemy. No game.*

"Wave goodbye," said Audrey's mom as they drove away from their emptied house, the rough road rumbling under their tires. Dad obeyed from the passenger seat, but Audrey's hands stayed tight in her lap as she stared out the window. She couldn't see the willow from this angle. This morning, she had visited one last time, but she hadn't been able to find the words for her feelings—not in Crow, not in human.

As her mom turned onto the highway, Audrey glimpsed a black silhouette in the air above their trees. Storm would find it soon, she hoped . . . the gummy worms and trail mix, and her craft kit open, the beads bright as gems.

DEATH AND LAUGHTER

Kaile Shilling

Kaile Shilling is the founder of the Arts for Incarcerated Youth Network (now the Arts for Healing and Justice Network), an organization dedicated to art and storytelling as a means to change both individuals and systems. She's worked in the film industry, and in social justice and juvenile justice reform efforts in Los Angeles, and is currently the Executive Director of the Vancouver Writers Fest. She lives in Vancouver, BC with her journalist husband, two kids, young dog, old cat, and three chickens. 'Death and Laughter' was chosen by judge Diana Gabaldon as an Honourable Mention for the Surrey International Writers' Conference 2021 Jack Whyte Storyteller's Award.

DEATH AND LAUGHTER

"How will we know?"

"Know what?" I reply.

"That she's gone?" Dad answers simply.

"She stops breathing," I respond. I remember when I had to put my cat to sleep, the final exhale, the stopping, and the weird shudder that followed, thirty seconds to a minute later, as the final pockets of air were pushed out by collapsed muscles.

After dinner he goes to the office in the barn, and I sit with Mom. When I was in high school, someone said once that when you can't do anything else, you can at least share silence with a person. That sharing silence, it is enough. It was, of course, in reference to some high school angst, but it stuck with me for decades. And it comes to me again now, as I sit in silence. Sharing silence with my mother. Grateful for years of Quaker meetings that taught me how. How to carry silence. How to share silence. And I realize, in the way that is only earned through time and living, that sharing silence is deep and profound and is simply sometimes all we can do. *Dayenu*, as my Jewish husband would say. It is enough.

My sister arrives, finally, from halfway around the world—somehow arriving the evening after the morning she left because time travel is real if you live enough time zones away.

I can't sleep. I get up once when I hear Dad struggling with Mom. She was trying to go to the bathroom and got as far as the chair. I talk to her calmly and firmly, in the voice I learned from her over years of growing up, the voice I heard her use on my own children when she'd come visit.

"We're going to go back to bed now, okay? I'm going to help you, and we're going to get you back in bed." We finally get her back in bed. Later I hear her again, and pad softly from my room to theirs. The door is open, and there I see Dad sitting up against the headboard, Mom lying crosswise on the bed. He is asleep, his head resting against his own shoulder, his legs pulled all the way up out of her way, as the soft glow of the low-hanging oversized paper globe casts them in warmth. They're not touching—I know he's afraid any touch might hurt her—and he has pulled himself utterly out of her way, yet it looks like she's draped across his lap. Like the Pietà inverted somehow, I think as I turn back to bed. The image burns in my heart. It is love.

My mother does not drink water again.

The next day we call the hospice number. They're going to send a one-to-one nurse, a crisis nurse. Someone who will sit in the room with her. It can't be long now, my sister and I think.

My husband and I talk later. He's visiting his family with our children. Our annual summer trip I skipped because some umbilical message told me to come here instead. They are scheduled to go back home to LA, but I know I'm here for the duration. Come here instead, I say. My dad has hundreds of thousands of airline miles. Now is the time to put them to use. My husband agrees, and it gives Dad a project for the day.

When the crisis care nurse arrives, she does an inspection of my mother. Not long, but possibly not soon. I try to tell her we are ready, that my mother is graceful and elegant and would want to leave us in a graceful, elegant way—not gasping ugly, desperate gasps at the last thin sliver of life, searching for the code that will let them know we want her to go. The nurse smiles. "It can be hard," she says, kindly. "You think you cannot bear it, but you can."

I want to scream at her, shake her, spell out what we are terrified to speak. What does she know, and why is she denying my mom rest when this is awful? I curse her Christian tattoo: "L.U.C.K.Y.—Living Under Christ's Kindness, Y'all." I think it's the *y'all*, with its southern self-assuredness and superiority, that offends me, almost as much as her refusal to read between the lines. But, I remind myself, this boundless compassion and belief in the miracle of life is also why this woman is here, in our home, at midnight, to sit with a stranger who is dying so that the family can sleep.

Her words come back to me several times. I think often that I have made peace, that I am in a good place, but then the end does not come. And then I find a deeper peace. And the floor just goes down and down. It is not, I realize, up to us to rush or decide. It will be clear when it happens, and we cannot rob my mom of her journey. If she is fighting, holding on, that is her choice too.

The nurse says that often the spouses check out. That they know their own limits. That this is fine. I am able to release my frustration and make more space for Dad to be absent from mom's bedside. Often, she continues, people do not die while their loved ones are in the room.

When you are there they have to hold on. When you are gone, they can let go.

Deane, one of my best friends from high school, comes again. By some miracle, he'd moved to West Virginia with his wife and is only a half-hour away from my parents' place that's far, far away from everyone else. The first time he came, a week ago, Mom had insisted he wait in the hall while she put on her wig. Then she asked him for the pot she knew he'd have to help with the nausea. He sits now, in the room, and my sister and I sit on the bed with Mom. He takes out his guitar.

He starts singing. My dad comes up and joins us. My sister eventually makes a space for him on the bed, and he comes around and sits on the side, taking Mom's hand.

It's the first time he's been able to do that. He hasn't been able to sit quietly in the room for two days. Mom beams at my dad through the music as he holds her hand.

She hasn't beamed at him unconditionally for a long time.

Miracles come in many forms. This is sometimes what they look like. A tone-deaf man, singing with my pothead friend from high school who has become a gorgeous musician, and holding the hand of his dying wife while she smiles. Somehow, all of us in the room shimmer.

The nurse, listening in the hall, asks for Deane's number with tears glistening. As if such magic can be replicated.

The surprising thing is how much beauty there is. Moments of grace and stunning kindness. I tell my sister part of it is that nobody needs anything from Mom anymore. No longer do we need to tell her anything, have her hear anything. We're just in a place of giving.

Tonight we sleep. For me, it's the first night I've really slept in a week. For Dad, who knows how long it's been, but we know he sleeps soundly in my sister's bed. My sister has come into my bed, and we chat and giggle like schoolgirls about silly things. It's addictive to laugh. We eventually fall asleep, both of us in the impossible place of hoping the night takes Mom away. Because we love her.

The morning light is soft and white. The mist still hovers, nestled among the hills. The sun is starting to light through the mist, illuminating the fog from within. There is more peace under the peace.

But things are not beautiful or peaceful. Things get ugly. Mom is breathing with her whole body. All her muscles are being used to help her breathe, the nurse tells us. Breath that would normally show in the gentle rise and fall of the tummy and chest is now an almost spasmodic effort that seems to use every ounce of failing energy she has left. She does not look peaceful or restful. It becomes almost intolerable. I declare that the kids — arriving tonight — will not set foot in the house.

We try to talk to Dad — we make it about him, a hypothetical. What if it were you, Dad? we plead. What would you want us to do? Mom's forced breath grinds over her vocal cords in the other room. He keeps telling us to flip the switch: he wouldn't want to be kept alive artificially.

There's no switch, I tell him, there's just a dosage. He does not understand.

"**You know what's** really stupid?" I ask my sister. "Fake boobs."

My sister spits her water across the room.

The perky little cupcakes still stand up cheerfully in mockery of my mother's wasted skeleton body, and the absurdity is frankly hilarious. Mom had always been small, with the breasts to match. Sometime in her sixties—possibly after the first cancer round—she got a boob job. From an A cup to a B cup. Not much, but just enough to annoy my sister and make me feel like my mom had betrayed every feminist, pro-your-own-body, anti-Barbie message she'd ever taught me. I'd told her so at the time. She'd insisted it was what she wanted, and poor Dad had just shaken his head, proclaiming that it obviously had never been a problem for him and, after forty-some years, certainly wasn't at his insistence. I forgot about it most of the time, but every once in a while when I hugged her and felt their unnatural firmness, I got a little flinch of anger about it.

The main hospice-team nurse, the British one, arrives about 11 a.m. She walks in, and her face registers surprise at Mom's condition. She immediately asks if we think Mom is in pain. Kaitlin and I—now understanding the code—nod vigorously. Dad asks how we would know if she was in pain.

The nurse tells me to give her a one-millilitre dose every four hours, instead of 0.25 every hour. She says this is Mom's new dosage, with an extra 0.5 to be given every hour in addition if we think it's needed. As I fill the syringe, I ask her pointedly if we will need to refill it. She confirms that we have enough to get through the day, and we don't need to worry about that right now.

I give Mom the dose. She does not open her eyes anymore, seems not to register anything. Half goes in one side of her mouth, half in the other, so as to minimize any that might drip out. She doesn't need to swallow it, the nurse confirms. It will be absorbed. This is the good stuff. Mom's breathing calms immediately. She stops moaning. Things relax in the room. The nurse confirms that a crisis care nurse will be here that afternoon. My sister and I head down to have lunch, leaving Dad in the room. Almost absent-mindedly, I remember to turn back. We're going down to have lunch, I tell my mother, sleeping on the bed. Then we'll be back. I love you, Mom. I kiss her hand.

It's like the end of pregnancy, I think. You are so hot and uncomfortable all the time that you don't care how bad labour is going to be — you just need to not be pregnant anymore. The next phase is no longer something to be feared, it is simply something to be done because the current condition is no longer tolerable. There is no more sentiment or tender lingering. There is just a need to have it accomplished.

Dad steps out of the room to talk on the phone. He paces in the hallway upstairs and eventually comes downstairs. It is somewhat unkind, I think, that my sister and I have stuck together and left him alone. It is a privilege to have a sibling in this. I head upstairs as my sister does the dishes.

I walk into the room and it is strangely calm. I see Mom, lying perfectly on the bed, calmer than she has been in hours. It takes me a few moments to realize that it's because she's no longer breathing. I stand, watching. Not believing. I kiss her gently on the head — a head whose hair long ago gave up trying to grow back — and she feels strange. I don't know if one can tell if a spirit has left a body, I just know that my mom is not there anymore.

I step out into the hallway and call my sister.

"Coming," she responds, and is up the stairs in moments. I nod at her from outside the room. We cry and hug. She says to wait before calling Dad, and gets the mouth swabs from the bathroom to clean up the bloody spittle out of the side of Mom's mouth. I hadn't noticed it, and I'm glad that she cleans Mom's cheek and neck, dabbing gently. "Oh, Mommy," she coos.

I go downstairs to my dad, who is sitting at the table, eating lunch. I hug him.

"She's gone," I say. He doesn't hear me. "Dad," I say louder, "she's gone." He stands and hugs me back.

"Oh, I'm so sorry," he says. "I'm so sorry." He is heading upstairs before I can ask if he wants to — I will quickly learn that he is not sentimental on this front. He wants to see and touch and understand. "How do you know?" he asks. "You can tell?" Upstairs, he sits on the chair next to her bed. He holds her hand. "I just don't understand how this happens," he says. "I think I still feel a little slight breath," he says. I shake my head. Given the full-body heaves she was doing before, there are no more slight breaths. He calls the hospice nurse.

The nurse arrives. She checks the heartbeat. "What time did she pass?" she asks. We have no idea and try to pinpoint the time between when my sister and I went down for lunch, when Dad was on the phone, and when we called out again to the hospice nurse. Sometime between 12:30 and 1:00 p.m.

"Twelve thirty-four," my sister declares. I look at her. "One two three four," she clarifies. "Mom likes whimsy."

We start making calls. The funeral home arrives. They are kind. Gentle and respectful, explaining what they will do and giving us permission to watch or not. They will give us final moments with her in the room, they explain. Then they will come up the stairs with the portable gurney, lift her onto it, bring her downstairs, set her and the portable gurney onto the rolling one, roll her into the back of the van, and drive off. Once they leave, they confirm, they will be done. No more paperwork, nothing else. We can come later to the funeral home to handle the rest of the details.

I tuck into a downstairs corner where I will not see. The merciful nurse waits downstairs with me. She hands me tissues and doesn't ask anything of me. Dad follows every step of the way. He asks for the bottom bed sheet to be returned after they transport her to the funeral home. My sister is incredulous.

"It's part of a set," he explains, unselfconsciously.

Eventually, it is time to head to the airport to pick up my husband and the kids. My dad wants to come, but I tell him he can't. I need to tell the kids my way, not his. I tell him my sister will come. I know this will leave him alone in the house, but I need support to manage this meeting. He is upset. It's the first time I've seen him get mad, even as mildly mad as it is. He wants to see the kids; besides, airport pickups are his job. This is when I realize that he loves greeting people at the airport. He loves being the first face of welcome, ushering folks home rather than waiting for them to arrive.

I put my foot down. For the first time on this trip, I am a mother first and a daughter second.

For the first time in my life, I am the only mom in the family. And just like that, just that fast, the generational cycle has turned, and I am the eldest woman in the family.

My sister and I arrive and park the car. We wait. I sway on my feet, tapping my foot. Finally, I see my children emerge.

My daughter in a sundress, hair matted from ten days with no mom to brush it. My little boy running behind her. I run towards them.

"Mommy, Mommy!" they squeal. I am tackled by their embrace, and the spell is broken. I hold them. Living, plump, soft, warm creatures.

The world exists again. Time starts. The haze and timelessness and endless quiet of the last days falls away.

There are tears as my seven-year-old comprehends what I'm telling her in a way my almost-four-year-old does not, but the dreaded first night in the house without Mom is suddenly filled with children, and noise, and their demands on our immediate attention. Mom's timing was always impeccable.

THE BUMBLEBEE FLASH FICTION CONTEST

THE BUMBLEBEE FLASH FICTION CONTEST

Flash fiction is swift and speedy, offering brief moments packed with zingy sweetness — or sharp stings. And the after-effects of the very best linger long.

This year's winner won over final judge Bob Thurber with *'the author's daring, and ability to control the rapid emotional flow with rhythmic insights'.*

Congratulations to first-place winner Christine Breede for 'Whispers in Between My Shoulder Blades', and to runner-up Cheryl Skory Suma for 'Adrift Off the Shore of Alzheimer Island'!

Thank you to all submitting authors. And congratulations to the short list:

Christine Breede for 'Whispers in Between My Shoulder Blades'
Shanda Connolly for 'My Daughter's Hair Stylist'
Stephanie Grella for 'Headfirst'
VJ Hamilton for 'Gut Feeling'
Lulu Keating for 'The Solution for Sleeplessness'
Shirlee Smith Matheson for 'Darts'
Alan Sincic for 'Count-Down'
Cheryl Skory Suma for 'Adrift Off the Shore of Alzheimer Island'
KT Wagner for 'Edible Flowers and Other Forage'

Christine Breede holds an MSc from Columbia University, serves as a speech therapist for the International School of Geneva, and organizes writers' workshops for teenagers and adults. Her work has been published online and in print, and has won several creative writing competitions. She was nominated for the 2020 Pushcart Prize and is currently at work on her first novel.

WHISPERS IN BETWEEN MY SHOULDER BLADES

BY CHRISTINE BREEDE

I have a friend who says, *I have morals, I don't do this or that,* and then she does, like when she wears her ring in every photograph, letting it shine, letting it weigh, until she takes it off for a couple of hours or doesn't, a minor detail at that point, and I have a friend who says, *Bear with it, it's a matter of expectations, you can still do this or that,* like the one who tells me, *We stopped making love and I might get a dog,* or the one who tells me, *I don't want to marry my partner, but if he'll leave me for that, I'll even marry him,* and another one who says, *My colleague makes me blush and my husband keeps me warm,* or the one who says, *We have our routine, every Sunday, because he likes it that way,* which could make you cringe or could mean you choose to be safe, choose to look away when you see the gleam in someone else's eyes, the mystery that makes me think of the friend who says, *After all these years, I feel crippled, less alive, but how much freedom can I bear, how do I listen to the whispers in between my shoulder blades,* or the friend who tells me, *I cannot carry that burden,*

I want someone else to carry me, be that light person again, and I wonder, I listen to all of them in awe, as if I couldn't be any one of them, waiting, weighing, until a friend sends me a text I cannot bear to delete, even though it haunts me, but I know if I delete it, I might also lose its promise, and it is as if I wrote it myself, once I stopped wishing things were as easy as wearing heart-shaped love glasses or hugging my child or taking a deep breath, once I stopped trying not to know what I already know and listened to the whispers in between *my* shoulder blades instead, reminding me of tenderness and the breath of love, not the shadow of right or wrong but the truth *and* the dare, once I am as brave as my friend says in the text I cannot delete, the one that says, *I am not worried about you, you know how a warm and tender touch in the dark can scare, and you let yourself be scared, you will always have love in your life.*

THE PLAY'S THE THING

Allison Bannister

Allison Bannister is a cartoonist and comics scholar with an MFA in Cartoon Studies and a PhD in Communication and Rhetoric. She writes and draws comics about ghosts, magic, and dinosaurs, tending toward stories about getting lost and finding a new way home. She teaches writing and visual storytelling. 'The Play's the Thing' is loosely based on her childhood amateur Shakespeare troupe, and was originally published in the Shakespeare tribute anthology My Kingdom for a Panel. Allison's graphic short 'Ghost Room' appears in Pulp Literature Issue 25, Winter 2020. You can find more of her work at basictelepathy.com.

Yeah, but it should still be sort of like the original.

He could try starving her--

--offer her soft bedding and take it away--

--think he's tamed her because she's sleep deprived and starving--

--and then she'll murder everyone!

I like it.

Ooh.

Yeah!

So, Petruchio takes on Kate as a favour to Bianca...

And I'll be like

do a trick!

Maybe we want someone to call out the abuse?

I could do that!

You're too shallow.

You want Kate gone so you can have a boooy frieend.

It could be one of Petruchio's servants--maybe he mistreats them too.

Can I play her instead?

Fine, I can play Bianca.

This is boring.

Let's do the part where everyone dies!

Do you wanna control Kate for that scene?

Yeah!

Maybe I secretly feed Kate when she's starving--

--she'll remember when she goes berserk!

Then we can both run away!

Ok, so in the next scene we need Bianca and Petruchio to hatch their plot.

Can I be eavesdropping?

Sure.

Petruchio, you must help me solve the problem of Kate, the shrew.

Fear not, Bianca!

I shall tame the shrew and claim her massive dowry.

Hey kids, it's time for the girls to go home.

We're rehearsing!

But Moooom!

Their parents called, it's time to go!

The casting call is murder

COMING SOON FROM

PULP LITERATURE PRESS

PRETTY LIES: HOLD ON

Mel Anastasiou

Mel Anastasiou *is a novel acquisitions and story editor with Pulp Literature Press, and she co-founded* Pulp Literature *magazine in 2013. Mel helps writers develop through her structural editing, the popular 'Writing Muse' Twitter feed, and two workbooks,* The Writer's Boon Companion: Thirty Days Towards an Extraordinary Volume *and* The Writer's Friend and Confidante: Thirty Days of Narrative Achievement. *Her fiction includes the Hertfordshire Pub Mysteries, the Monument Studio Mysteries, and the Stella Ryman Mysteries, for which she won a Literary Titan Gold book award and was longlisted for the Leacock Medal.*

$\mathcal{H}$OLD ON

It's the golden summer of 1974 on Bowen Island, BC. Inspired by the story of Orpheus and Euridice, Jenny Riley searches for re-entry into the ghost world to bring back her dead love, Joey. These attempts put her and others in mortal danger, and Jenny's search is increasingly threatened by the ghost of Moira, who presses upon Jenny her own agenda for life after death.

CHAPTER 12

Jenny saw the car, the same black car that had hit her not half an hour before, turn off the trunk road and cut through the line-up for the ten-thirty ferry into the general store parking lot. She had lost sight of young Ketchup and his bag of chips but heard the driver's wordless shout and the wallop of the Eldorado's brakes.

She ran across the road and narrowly missed being hit herself by an orange pickup. Malcolm passed her, breathing hard, followed by Adrian, who apparently did care about kids after all. The driver clambered out, but there was no sign of Ketchup.

Malcolm tore up to the Eldorado's driver and shoved him in the chest.

"Bastard," Malcolm said. "I knew you were a bastard."

"I didn't do *anything*. Where's the kid?"

Jenny ran around the black car. She expected to see the little boy lying smashed and dead under the wheels, but she found him alive, stretched out on the parking lot blacktop.

"I'm crying because I'm hurt," Ketchup told her. His eyes moved to Adrian at Jenny's side. "No eating my chips."

Ketchup's left leg lay at an odd angle. But was that all? She knew better than many that more than bones could be broken on a person who'd been hit by a car. Something damaged deep inside would be harder to find, and the harder to find, the more dangerous it was. Did it follow that imagined injuries could be the most dangerous of all? She grimaced. Idiotic thoughts ran through one's head at a moment like this.

A crowd had gathered in the general store parking lot, largely from the line of parked cars waiting for the ferry.

"Call the ambulance."

"Is there one? On this punk island?"

"There's a service. There has to be."

"Turn him on his side."

"Don't turn him! He's breathing …"

"Take the chip bag away. He'll choke on them."

Adrian's voice was unmistakable in the crowd. "If you want to take his chips, you'll have to run him over again first."

More folks arrived in the parking lot, and Jenny found herself pushed aside by strong arms. A voice sounding accustomed to giving orders called, "Back up and leave a circle. The ambulance is coming."

Jenny pressed forward and saw that Chief Layton, neck wet with sweat above his white collar, was taking charge of the emergency.

Chief Layton bent over Ketchup. "You're the fire maker, aren't you? I knew you were a brave boy."

Ketchup's lower lip quivered. "I'm crying again."

"You hold onto those chips, son, and you'll be fine." Chief Layton got to his feet. "Is anyone else hurt here? What about the driver?"

"I'm the driver." The Eldorado's driver had tears in his eyes, Jenny saw. She wasn't sure whether this meant he was a villain or not. It had always seemed to her that villains—like Joey's friend Lerner, for example—had a pretty positive view of themselves, but nobody could feel good about knocking down small boys. "I'm not hurt."

A woman in the crowd called, "What about the passenger in the black Eldorado?"

"The driver was alone." That was Malcolm, on the far side of Ketchup.

"No, he had a girl in the seat beside him." This from Tanaka, one of the campers. Jenny looked down at his serious eyes and the slim alder branch trailing from his hand.

A woman with a turned-down mouth said, "The kid's right. There was a young woman in the car, and she should have stopped him."

Chief Layton asked, "What did the girl look like? Is she here now?"

"There was no girl in my car," the driver protested. "I was alone."

"Let me take your information." Chief Layton felt in his pockets and pulled out a pencil stub and a bit of paper.

Malcolm said, "This guy just hit Jenny with the same car."

Jenny felt unexpectedly sorry for the man in the black Eldorado.

People kept stepping out of nowhere in front of his car as if asking to be hit. Ketchup from the general store, and Jenny from … *where? I was there, and now I'm here.* She touched the side of her leg, where her skin showed no mark at all. To be honest, she was no longer certain that she'd ever been hit at all, any more than she was certain she'd been at Lerner's party in the ghost world. She wasn't sure of anything that she'd seen or done since Moira's advent. "I'm fine," she told Chief Layton.

Chief Layton said to the driver, "Well, of course the police will want to interview you. Breathe on me."

The driver leaned over and puffed in Chief Layton's face.

Chief winced. "You haven't been drinking, or not that I can tell. Anyway, go prove that to the police. Then bring the officers back here."

Malcolm grunted, "I'll get the police. I don't trust him to get them himself."

Chief Layton shook his head. "Let the driver go for the police. He feels bad, and you can't go far from the law on an island anyway, not without driving into the sea."

From the dock at the bottom of the hill, the ferry whistle blew.

Chief Layton turned to the gathered spectators. "The ferry's leaving in five minutes, everybody, and the island ambulance loads first."

The crowd dispersed towards their cars. Jenny touched the sleeve of the woman who had spoken earlier. "*Was* there a girl in the car?"

The woman shrugged. "Don't know anymore. You know, the little boy's going to be …"

"Okay?" Jenny asked. She stared at the woman. And at that inopportune moment, Jenny received, as if by telegraph, a memory of the night Joey died. When help had arrived at the scene of the crash, she'd looked up from the passenger seat of the mangled yellow Zed to see the policeman lay his hand on Joey's golden head beside her. Jenny had waited for the policeman to say those exact words: *The boy's going to be okay. The boy's going to be fine.* But he hadn't. What was it that the policeman had said about Joey?

Two words. She strained to recall them.

Frances's green Galaxie roared down the Cove hill and stopped with a clunking noise in the middle of the road beside the ferry queue. A battered ambulance pulled around her and nosed into the parking lot.

Frances climbed out of the Galaxie and stormed up to Jenny. "A neighbour phoned. Did you get yourself hit by a car?"

"Yes, she did," Malcolm said.

"Not really," Jenny said. "But Ketchup was knocked down."

"Dear God, what next?" Frances held up a hand in greeting to the emergency crew, both men long-haired and wearing jeans. Ketchup lay flat on his back and held his bag of chips away from the ambulance men as they unrolled a stretcher and lifted him onto it.

"You'll have to go with the boy." Frances dug into her pocket. "Take my car."

"I thought you said I couldn't drive." Jenny reached for the keys.

"Not *you*— you." Frances jerked her head at Malcolm. "*You* look reliable. Although you also look soft. If she asked you, would you let Jenny take the car?"

"Yes," Malcolm said.

"No, you would not. Do you promise?"

"Yes."

"Huh."

The men shifted Ketchup onto a trolley and into the rear of the ambulance. Chief Layton climbed up front.

"I'm not your mother," Frances said to Jenny. "I won't even try to protect you from yourself. But I want another promise."

Jenny looked at her feet. "What now?"

Frances put her cheek near Jenny's and spoke into her ear. "Do you want me to ask it out loud? Just promise you'll come back in one piece."

Jenny looked after the ambulance as it pulled away. It was vital that she go to the hospital on the mainland with Ketchup, although she couldn't have explained why. She couldn't even have made up a believable lie. Her heart pounded so hard that it hurt. "I promise, all right?"

Adrian ambled up and hung an arm around Malcolm's shoulder. "He'd better promise to be careful, too, because you wouldn't want to put a dent in that mint Galaxie 500 of yours."

Frances said, "You must be the sarcastic one. Adrian. Yes, my car's a disaster. Happy? Good. Now listen to me, Adrian. Phone the camp and make them get hold of Ketchup's parents. Then you will look after all these campers, because it's not my responsibility. It's yours." She took Adrian by the shirt and dragged him to the pay phone by the store, where he pulled himself free of her and lifted the receiver while she pushed a coin into the slot.

Jenny climbed into the passenger seat of the Galaxie, and Malcolm steered them to the back of the line of cars and onto the ferry. Once on board, Jenny slammed out of the car and headed for the bow of the ferry, where the ambulance sat with its rear door open. The emergency team chatted and smoked by the big ashtray near the stairs. Jenny approached the ambulance to find Ketchup on his stretcher, craning to look out at the cars.

"You're so brave," Jenny told him. Ketchup frowned and cradled his bag of chips.

"We covered him with a blanket," one of the long-haired emergency team said. "We promised him pizza."

"Everybody lies," Ketchup said. "Everybody except Jenny, I bet."

Jenny perched on the ambulance floor with her feet hanging outside. She watched Ketchup attempt to keep his eyes open, lose the struggle, and sleep. She rested her palm on his blanket. Beside her own, another hand reached out to touch the blanket that covered Ketchup.

Jenny looked up into Moira's eyes. Moira looked away.

"Did you do this? Were you in the car?" Jenny demanded.

"A person can go for a ride, I guess."

"And harm a little boy?"

"*I* wasn't driving, was I? Of course I wouldn't hurt him. I'll be a mother myself someday," Moira said over the sleeping boy. "Poor kid."

Jenny leaned back against the open ambulance door. Oh, yes, she thought. Now I remember. Two words that the policeman had said over Joey in the wreck of the yellow Zed. *Poor kid.*

"Somebody saw you in the Eldorado with the driver," Jenny said.

"Somebody needs glasses, then," Moira replied. "Are you coming?"

Jenny blinked. "I'm not coming anywhere, except with Ketchup and Malcolm to the hospital."

"You've always got a reason to leave me flat," Moira said. "Well, sister, this is the best excuse so far. But don't be long, will you?"

Moira didn't pause for Jenny's answer. She climbed up onto the steel boat rail on the starboard side of the ferry and vanished over the edge.

CHAPTER 13

Moira leapt with conscious grace down from the ferry boat rail to the Bowen Island Hotel dance floor. She rose with a swish of skirts and looked around for Philip. He wasn't waiting for her here, where the old women sat with balls of wool in their laps and needles between their fingers. They glanced her up and down, and she looked past them into the centre of the crowd of dancers, pairs locked together while a slow song played.

Moira turned her back on her elders and brushed past the swaying, tight-packed couples towards the source of the music. In the centre of the room, the bandleader crooned into his microphone, *"Moonlight and roses become you."*

What a waste of a slow song, with Philip not yet in her arms or, indeed, anywhere to be seen among the dancers. Didn't the bandleader know any other tunes? Didn't he know something jazzy? A dancer backed into her and nearly knocked her down, which reminded her of the little boy with the broken leg back on the boat. But he would be fine, and safe soon with his parents. She murmured to herself, "When Philip and I have children of our own, I'll twirl them round and sing to them until they laugh and we all fall down."

She felt a light touch upon her sleeve.

"What about a dance with the man of your dreams?"

And so here was Philip at last. She turned to wrap her arms around him and to take a strip off him, in that order, because she hadn't seen him for what seemed like a lifetime. But when she turned, it wasn't Philip after all. This was only a red-headed sad sack she'd never laid eyes on in all her born days.

He'd be a little bit cute, though, if it weren't for that nose.

"Go away," she sang at him over the real lyrics of the love song. "I'm in love and not with you."

He wrinkled that nose. "And yet here's a pretty girl like you, dancing alone."

If I'm so pretty, then where's Philip? It made her want to spit.

The bandleader waved his stick and pulled at his white dinner jacket, a little grey around the cuffs. Still, the words of his song were sweet.

"Dance with me, since I'm your dream invention," the fellow said. "Tell yourself I'm here to make that Joe of yours jealous. Best of all, put your cheek against mine."

"Fresh." Where was Philip? The dancers churned around the floor. Like Moira and the redhead, most were neatly dressed in pale colours suitable for a summer night. However, they trailed smells of sweat and hair oil. And their manners left something to be desired. For instance, a young man dancing next to her, wearing an unfashionable but appealing too-long blond haircut, leaned over his partner's shoulder and winked at her.

Over at the edge of the dance floor, the line of old women with their folded mouths sat in a row and gave her the old knitting-needle stare. Moira didn't care. *I'll never be old like them*, she told herself. It was not, somehow, a comforting thought.

She shivered and eyed her own partner. His nose wasn't so bad. "You break your schnozz fighting over a girl?" she asked him.

"I'd fight for you," the redhead said. "My sometimes-girlfriend is a nurse, and she'll take care of any wounds I might incur."

"You're quite the two-timer." Moira was enjoying the repartee. "But your nurse doesn't have to worry, because I'd never go for a redhead."

"Too bad. Still, isn't it fun thinking what your fella would say if he saw you dancing close to me?"

"Philip knows I'm true."

"Of course you are."

At these words, she relented and touched her cheek to his. His hand brushed her behind.

She smacked his ear. "That bank's closed," she told him.

She led for a few steps just to teach him. He chuckled, let go of her, and disappeared into the crowd. She stood alone on the floor amid the dancing couples until somebody tapped her shoulder. She met the gaze of the blond fellow with the too-long hair and the untucked shirt.

He asked, "Looking for me?"

"Everybody's so confident tonight," she complained. "I'd appreciate some male bashfulness around here."

"How's this? Let's walk around the floor a little, if you think you can endure me."

She could; he smelled better than most.

He pulled Moira against his chest and pressed his cheek against hers without so much as a *can I buy you a drink*. She knew his type now. This was just the kind of light-fingered Freddy who'd undo your brassiere for you, and you'd never notice until things started to slip. She didn't know where these men purchased the nerve.

She said, "Hands off, handsome. For the sake of my future children."

"You feel good in my arms," he said. "Good thing I learned the foxtrot in gym class. I like this kind of slow dancing, body to body."

"Don't get too friendly."

"Just averagely friendly. Do you want to know a secret?"

"I always want to know a secret." Moira dared a finger under the loose hem of his shirt. She touched the skin at his back. He felt warm. It was only when he held her close this way that she wondered why she'd felt cold so long.

He grinned, and Moira returned her hand to his shoulder.

"Here's the secret," he said. "You know how for most people, there are good moments and then there are bad moments?"

"I guess so." She remembered throwing a glass at Philip once, but she'd been drunk and he'd been acting cold-hearted.

"With me, it's all good moments, Moira."

"You must be a magician, then." Had she told him her name? She couldn't remember. "What's *your* name?" she asked.

He shrugged. "I'm just your average Joe," he said. "My good moments involve my buddies, my girl, and a well-stocked party house. I bet yours are about the same, right?"

"Listen, you. I want to know your secrets, not tell mine."

The average Joe squeezed her tight, and she let him press her against his chest. She pretended he was Philip and mused on what life held in store for her as it did for all the lucky women in the world: a man that suited her, her own kitchen, and children napping in a window seat while she heated milk for them on a new enamelled stove. These thoughts should have been happy ones, but, oddly, she wanted to cry. She felt a sudden panic, as if time were passing her by. As if it had, in fact, passed, and a glance in a mirror would show her an old woman like the crones at the edge of the dance floor. No husband, no children.

She turned her face up, and the blond Joe looked into her eyes with an odd sort of expression. It must have been admiration. He couldn't be laughing at her.

She said, "A penny for them."

"I'm wondering whether we're alike in other ways, you and me. I'll bet both of us are the jealous kind."

"That's a little bit interesting. Who are you jealous of?"

"The fellow who's after my girl. You?"

She wasn't about to tell this fellow about Philip.

Joe held her close with one hand and held something up in the other. She hadn't noticed him pick up a glass of something to drink, but here it was: a green glass full of something dark.

She'd seen a drink like that before, and not so long ago. It looked pretty dire, but it was wet, and she had a thirst the size of a whale. "Gimme."

He gave her. She tipped it back, drank. It tasted like bitter power, like the best two-dollar rum in the world.

She handed the glass back to him. She'd left a mouthful in the bottom. He toasted her with it. "To the end, my friend."

That was a new one on her. She liked his way with words. Maybe Philip could go hang. The thought made her bite her lip. She felt hot all over. The *idea* of it.

She left the average Joe to the last drops in his green glass and elbowed a path away from him through the crowd. He wouldn't follow her.

He wouldn't dare.

But he did. "Leave Jenny alone."

"Don't waste your breath, Joe. Save it to thank me for the dance." Moira pushed past a couple of latecomers and left the dance hall. It was black outside in the shadows of the trees, but she was sure as death and taxes that she could track down Jenny, wherever she was or whatever she was doing.

CHAPTER 14

Back at home on her porch after a dusty half-hour's walk from the cove, Frances Riley assumed she was alone in her bay. Out in front of her house, the sea shone as flat as a silver tray. The sky over Gambier Island across the Sound was so blue that on such a morning she could almost forget that winter had ever happened, that poverty and war girdled the globe, and that kids got hit by cars. She could even forget there were professional rivals like her fellow archaeologist Gig Chalmers in the world. But the St Albans dig was hers, and the mosaic was as good as uncovered, every tile clean as the day it was laid in Emperor Trajan's time.

Frances folded herself into her deck chair and counted the cost of having put off her flight to Heathrow so as to include Jenny in the trip. She'd offered up her valued and cranky solitude to Owen's difficult daughter. Did this act balance her debt to Owen's side of the family? For, long ago in the grey dawn of Frances's eighth birthday, she'd stood at her mother's side on Owen's parents' doorstep, holding tight to her suitcase and trying to hide her mother's blood on her coat sleeve. "Can we come in?" her mother had asked Owen's father, like a drowning woman. "May we stay?" They'd stayed for good.

No, the debt to her relatives remained unpaid. Frances sighed. *Family.* No wonder that once she grew up, she lived alone. With family, nothing was enough and everything was too much. And just try to keep people safe. Reference her mother's blood at her father's hand. After which, her mother had lived and her father had died. Honestly, you needed a scorecard in life in order to calculate your chances of survival, let alone happiness. And even then, you could only count on one thing: even fortune's favourites didn't get out alive.

The porch shook. A pair of hands wrapped themselves around the railing, and a long-legged young man swung himself up and onto her deck. The sunlight was so strong that she had to squint to see his face, but she recognized him as Adrian, the counsellor she'd bullied into phoning the camp to get in touch with the injured camper's parents. Now he stood over her, breathing hard and giving her a look she hadn't seen since she'd failed a couple of first-year students for plagiarism the semester before.

"Hello," she said. "Please get off my porch, and take care of your kids as discussed."

"What kids? I don't see any kids." He leaned back against the railing and crossed his arms. "I'm here to ask you a favour."

"Consider it denied. I've been teaching long enough to recognize the type who turns favours for you into big mistakes for me." Frances suspected something else about him as well. She sat up a little taller and shielded her eyes with one hand. Weed, of course. And maybe those dull little orange pills you bought in alleys, that students called Sunshine. "Watch yourself. I know all about you kids today, walking around with your shirts untucked, stoned out of your minds. But your kind of young person has been around since the dawn of time. The ancient Essenes complained about the addictions of their young people. The poet Coleridge was always getting high, and everybody knew it. Youth always thinks there's something new under the sun."

"I guess you know everything, then." He shoved his fists into his pockets.

Frances made an effort to relax her shoulders.

"Do I make you nervous, Miss Riley? I hope not."

"*Doctor* Riley." His good manners were a little frightening when you contrasted them with the fists in his pockets. "Or *Professor* Riley. I can see that you're determined to ask me for that favour, and as you're too heavy for me to strong-arm off my property, ask and be done with it."

"I want you to go after Jenny and make her come back here with you."

"Why?"

"I don't want her hanging around with that Malcolm fellow."

"Why not?"

"She's meant to be with me. As the whole world knows."

"Why you and not Malcolm?"

He laughed. "Ask Jenny. Ask her anytime in the course of her life whether it isn't me she's meant to be with."

"You're getting a bit ahead of yourself, aren't you? You hardly know her, Adrian."

"What did you call me?" He blinked his green eyes, and the sunlight lit the tips of his lashes.

Frances had long ago recognized the complete lack of connection between integrity and good looks, at least outside of fairy tales. "I got the name right, didn't I? You're Adrian."

"Am I?"

"Aren't you?" She blinked up at him. For the first time she wondered whether the sun in her eyes hadn't blinded her to the possibility that this wasn't Adrian at all, that Adrian was somewhere else entirely. And if so, who was this young man who was so like him that they could have been siblings?

"If you're not him, then kindly tell me who you are."

"I'll tell you one thing, Dr Riley. And listen closely. There's not a force in the world that can come between a young woman and her true love."

"Ask Ophelia what she thinks about that." Frances skirted away from any mention of Orpheus. "Anyway, you've got it just a little bit wrong."

"Wrong?" He frowned.

"Yes. Here's the truth of it." She spoke with care. "Not even death can make a stubborn young woman break up with her no-good boyfriend."

"Huh. That's a pretty bold thing to say to me. Since you're so full of truth, come on and make Jenny see reason."

"Come where, exactly?"

"Just step over the line and find out."

"What line?" Frances asked, but there it was in front of her: a shadow, cast by nothing that she could see, cutting across the planks of her deck. She was on one side of it; he was on the other. She had no intention of crossing the shadow line, but her feet moved anyway, seemingly on their own. She followed him off her deck and onto the bluff above Corner Bay.

His hair glowed like an undeserved halo.

He jumped down the black rocks to the water, where he moved up to his waist and pushed deeper. He appeared to be heading directly out into the moving waters of the Sound. He was only up to his chest now, and this was extraordinary, because the water was deep enough in that part of a bay to anchor a speedboat. How did he stay dry from his chest to the top of his head?

Frances moved deeper in his traces, feeling her way. The water around her hips was as green as a frog's back and so clear that when she looked down she saw her brown legs and the bed of the bay, even browner and patterned with stones. A small crab skittered across her left foot. She took another step, and another. She was up to her shoulders now. As a child she loved to sink down and let the water close over her head. She'd look up past the surface at the sun and wave her arms in semi-circles, wondering at the white lines that traced the sun's refracted rays. She'd struggle to stay under, making big bubbles out of her breath and watching them rise.

The blond fellow, up to his neck in the bay and full of himself as ever, turned to face her. He said, "You're too slow. I'll fetch Jenny by myself."

She moved forward, but sunlight flashed on the water, and she lost sight of him. She took another step out into the bay. How she loved the water.

CHAPTER 15

Malcolm had been waiting with Jenny for an hour in the reception area of Lions Gate Hospital, and he didn't like the smells. He didn't like the uniforms or the nurses wearing them. Above all, he resented that he was once again *responsible*—for Ketchup and for Jenny. Responsibility without power, the ultimate rip-off.

From a glass cubicle nearby, a nurse eyeballed the two of them. Malcolm read her nameplate. *Georgia.* He wondered whether her father was named George, and if being named after a male parent negatively affected her. Over by the ladies' room door, a sign read, *Don't come empty-handed ... bring flowers.* He wondered whether people read the sign and did buy some flowers, or whether the dig at their manners just made them mad. Questions without answers, the penultimate rip-off.

Malcolm threw himself down beside Jenny on the reception couch. "Why would they use a nurse at the reception desk? Isn't that a waste of medical training?"

"Maybe they need her to sort people out. To eyeball them. Triage, isn't that the word?"

"In Emergency, yes. In Reception, no." Malcolm breathed in yet another lungful of medicinal-tasting air. "My parents want me to be a doctor."

"Why?"

Because I'm so responsible.

"Because I'll make a lot of money and help people." He imagined that sometimes he sat up in bed and said this in his sleep.

"Which part of that don't you like?"

He wondered whether she was interested or only pretending and decided he didn't care. "I'm twenty-two, and already I'm tired of helping people. Especially kids."

She smiled. "What a hero you are."

"I guess I wouldn't mind being the guy that fixed people. But what about the ones you couldn't fix?" Jenny shot him a glance that read pure startlement. Probably she hadn't thought much about the people who died in the hospital. "Anyway, they wouldn't bring dying people through Reception. Those would come in through Emergency. Old age. Cancer. Car crashes."

"I hate this hospital too. I had a friend who died here." The look in Jenny's grey eyes cut him somewhere deep down. "Listen, I've been wondering. I've had a bad time today, and it might be my fault for not letting go of something that happened to me. A few somethings. What if I just gave up and let everything go?"

How could a person let everything go? He wanted to tell her that it was not possible to let go of everything, because everything had you tight around the neck and would never release you.

He stood up and moved towards the elevators. "I wish Ketchup's parents would come down and talk to me so we can finish up here. I've got a little money, and we could get burgers."

Jenny held out her hand. "Give me the keys to Frances's Galaxie."

"I promised her not to let you drive."

"I'm not going to drive the car. I just want to get my sweater. I'm cold."

Pale as porcelain now, she'd never looked less pretty. "What sweater?"

"My blue sweater, the one in the car."

He couldn't remember a sweater, but he would hardly have noticed with Frances's clutter in the back seat. "I'll get it."

"Don't." Against all expectation, Jenny stepped up to him as close as kissing and slipped a hand into the back pocket of his shorts. She fished for the keys.

They stood face to face, him looking down and her up. He could feel her hands in his pockets, and he remembered how he used to envy those guys whose girlfriends walked with their hands deep in their boyfriends' back pockets. He'd thought it would feel warm and intimate, and he'd been right.

He leaned down. He leaned down and kissed her. He kissed her as if he were some other, braver guy, the hero type. Jenny's eyes closed and opened, like a doll's.

She said, "Damn."

"Not good?"

"I didn't say that. I just said *damn*."

Jenny turned and walked away, Frances's car keys dangling from her hand. She pushed through the glass doors that opened to the street. As she passed under the trees lining the sidewalk, she looked like a shadow, not a living thing at all. She disappeared around the corner where he'd parked the Galaxie, off Lonsdale Avenue, out of sight.

She'd be back in a moment. For a number of years now he'd felt as if he'd been waiting for his life to start, and when she came back, it would.

Malcolm stood in a state of wonder by the glass doors of the reception area. His blood buzzed through his circulatory system, and when the receptionist gave him an ironic look, he didn't care.

How long would it take Jenny to find the key, open the Galaxie door, and pull out her sweater? Even taking into consideration the debris in the back seat, it shouldn't take this long. He pictured her beside the car. In his imagination she'd dropped the keys onto the street between the curb and the car, and she was crying. He hadn't known how to answer when Jenny said she needed to let go of everything. And he understood her statement no better than before. But, rooted to the floor near the reception desk and waiting for Jenny to return, he did come to appreciate the import of a hundred love songs he'd heard on the radio.

"Malcolm?"

He spun around at the sound of his name. Ketchup's parents stepped out of the elevator. Ketchup's dad scrubbed with his hand at a splotch of darker blue on his shirt against which Ketchup—or his mother—must have wept.

Before he did anything else, Malcolm needed to sit down with them, to tell them all he'd seen in the parking lot when their son had been hit by a car. He would let them know exactly what had transpired. He owed them that. Ketchup had been hurt on Malcolm's watch. Also, it was his job. And one thing Malcolm knew was that you did the job.

"He's going to be okay," Ketchup's father said.

Malcolm shook their hands. "Great. That's terrific news."

"What exactly happened in the parking lot? Something to do with chips …"

"He ran away, and I was a minute too late catching up with him. I'd have thrown myself in front of that damned Eldorado if I could've."

… ran away, and I was a minute too late. Malcolm's heartbeat sped up. He said, "Look, I'm up to my ears in déjà vu. Call the camp director. I'm glad Ketchup's okay."

Malcolm left Ketchup's parents in front of the elevators. He tore through the hospital reception doors and along the sidewalk, running along the length of the hospital towards the side street where he'd parked Frances's Galaxie. He was seeing his third vision of extreme danger in as many hours. How was it that on this particular day he had transformed into a person who knew what was going to happen? Was he gaining experience, or was the world becoming more dangerous? It hardly mattered, because what it came down to was this: he would save her. His girl. Jenny. He felt sure that she was at the brink of some unguessable, difficult choice. Her qualities, which he had so recently found unreasonable and extreme, he now saw as the signs of a young woman at the breaking point. He swore to himself he'd help her back from whatever sharp edge she stood poised upon, alone over a great blue drop.

Malcolm turned the corner and looked ahead to where the Galaxie should have been, trusting to his instinct that Jenny would be leaning against the car as he'd foreseen her, in all her tragic beauty. Instead he ran through an empty space and out into the street, where he stopped between two black burn marks on the road.

Jenny might not have left those marks. A speeding stranger in a different car could easily have left them, tearing off in a shriek of burning rubber, headed west. Malcolm didn't know anymore. In fact, he didn't know much of anything.

There was a guy leaning up against a nearby tree, and Malcolm asked him, "Did you see a girl in a Galaxie?"

The guy laughed. His face was in shadow, but his posture, combined with that laugh, reminded Malcolm of Adrian in a mocking mood, and nobody needed to be laughed at by two guys like Adrian. Malcolm wanted to walk away without another word, but he needed an answer.

"A girl. Sure." The guy lifted one shoulder and let it fall again. Even shadowed as he was, his blond hair appeared to be damp, as if he'd just come from the beach or the pool. "But you see a lot of those, don't you?"

"She's gone."

"Too bad."

"I don't know what to do."

"Don't you? If I had to guess, you're going to attempt to bird-dog somebody else's girlfriend. Good luck with that." The guy laughed again and walked off towards Lonsdale.

After all, Malcolm discovered that he did know what to do. He'd kissed Jenny, so he knew what to do, hero or no hero, car or no car. Malcolm ducked under a branch that shadowed the sidewalk and began walking west, towards the bus stop and the distant ferry terminal where he was seventy-eight percent certain Jenny was heading.

Chapter 16

Frances stood on tiptoe, up to her neck in Corner Bay. She used a sweeping motion with both arms to keep herself upright. The yellow-haired youth had vanished like a flash of sunlight on water. She took another step out into the bay so that the water washed up to her ears. Her mind felt fuzzy, and she couldn't remember why she was following him, only that she wished to. Maybe if she pushed out a little deeper, she'd catch sight of him again above the swell of Howe Sound waters.

A noisy splashing declared itself from shore. She paddled herself around to face the approaching kerfuffle, and, in a turning as unexpected as a stranger's kiss, she found herself afflicted by small children. Three boys in yellow T-shirts and dirty shorts waded through the shallows towards her, huffing and swearing at the cold water.

"Hey lady, wait for us."

"Don't come out here, damn it all."

The tallest boy pushed out in front of the other two, into the centre of the bay, hands above his head and water up to his shoulders. The second one, the smallest, approached with his chin up to keep his face out of the water. He squirmed out of his shirt, laid it across the surface of the water, and sank it with his fist.

He said, "You shouldn't swear in front of kids. Even though we know all the words."

Frances frowned. "Look, don't come any deeper. Where's your counsellor?"

"Adrian vamoosed into town, and we're glad he did," the taller one said. "We don't want any more counsellors."

A third boy caught up to them. "They never let us do anything at this stupid camp." He set to splashing the first two in the efficient manner Frances remembered employing as a child, wherein the power of the splash proceeded from the heel of the hand. Frances wiped salt water from her eyes. What was she doing out here in the middle of her bay? That blond fellow must have cast some sort of spell over her, and the issue she had never previously considered regarding spells was that you might not want to escape them. Sleeping Beauty was probably happy getting her solid hundred years of shut-eye.

"Hey, you kids." The boys' heads turned in the water and floated there, disembodied. Regarding her. Waiting for her question. She was glad she'd never known what it was like to be a mother. She guessed one was ignored, condescended to, and rebelled against, when all one was doing was trying to keep them safe. I'm not a parent; I'm a professor, she thought. Even children of this age must respect a teacher.

She said, "I want to ask you boys an important question. And no baloney from you, either."

They swivelled to face her. The littlest one sank slightly and blew bubbles. She gave him the teacher's eye. "I mean it. I teach adults at the university, and I don't have a lot of patience for squeezing sensible answers out of eight-year-olds. First, tell me your names."

They told her. *Two-Can, Flash, and Tanaka.* She rolled her eyes.

"Honey, you can't love seven," Tanaka sang, bobbing up over a small wave and down again. *"You can't love seven and still go to . . ."*

Frances gave Tanaka the look again. "Stop bobbing and answer my question. How do your parents keep you safe?"

Tanaka kept bobbing, but he answered. "We have to promise stuff. Like don't run after balls into the street." He dropped fully under the surface.

Frances decided he could stay under there all day as far as she was concerned, or at least she would take no action until he'd been underwater a minute and a half. Then she'd have to save him. Like a lifeguard. Like a mother.

Flash blew water out through his nose. "We have to promise not to get into cars with murderers. That kind of promise. To keep us *safe.* They tell us stuff like that all the time."

"All the time." Tanaka resurfaced and made fish mouths at her.

"Right. I see," Frances said. "So, let's say you'd promised to . . ." What would children of this age have to promise? She couldn't imagine.

"Like, we have to stay out of the water unless we're wearing a lifejacket." That was Two-Can, the biggest one.

". . . or unless there's a lifeguard."

"We had to promise *that* or we couldn't come to camp."

They bobbed up and down, Tanaka moving in a circle.

Frances bobbed a little herself, just to try. "You're in the water right now without a lifejacket. You broke your promise."

There was the same sort of veiled contempt in Two-Can's gaze that she saw in some of her peers at department meetings. "You gotta promise to do stuff they tell you to do. Even if it's stupid. Even if you're not going to do it. If you don't promise, they stick you in your room."

"So you tell lies?" Frances frowned. Jenny had promised to look after herself. Was it possible that such promises were worth nothing? Was that why the world was filled with lawyers and heartbreak?

Flash snorted. "Sure, we lie, or we'd never get to do anything we want."

So how did you keep someone safe? She'd confine Jenny to Corner Bay if she had to. She'd feed her tranquilizers and drag her unconscious but alive onto the plane to England.

With a start, she counted only two young faces gazing owlishly at her. Where was that littlest boy? Tanaka. How long had he been under this time?

Tanaka surfaced, grinning, a line of snot running from his nose. "I petted a whale," he said.

He told this lie so prettily that she wanted to drown him. When do most of us stop being such good liars? Frances asked herself. When we grow too coarsely large to be cute about it? To the children, she said, "Hey! What about keeping somebody in their room, does that work?"

"Well …" Two-Can floated onto his back and started kicking up a storm. He shouted, "It teaches them a good lesson."

"Yes, it teaches them how to get out of their room so nobody knows," Flash agreed.

Frances turned towards shore. "I have to go somewhere, and I can't take you. Get out of the water now."

"Nope," Tanaka said. All three submerged.

"It's a matter of life and death," she told the empty surface of the water. "I can't wait for you kids."

Two-Can came up holding out a yellow pebble. "Pay me a million dollars, and I'll give you this pearl."

Frances, who couldn't wait, nonetheless waited for the other two boys to surface and herded them with painful slowness towards shore.

Chapter 17

Jenny drove through North Vancouver's light midday traffic, heading for the ferry terminal. The highway westward turnoff lay just ahead at the top of Lonsdale, a couple of minutes away. She gripped the wheel of Frances's car, her hands at ten and two o'clock as she'd learned in Drivers' Ed. Cars flashed from one lane to the next, red, brown, and green, darting like fish.

She imagined Joey as he used to sit, reclined and impatient in the passenger seat, one foot atop the dashboard. Reaching over to play with the turn signals. She'd bat his hand away and they'd laugh. She said to the empty seat beside her, "I'll drive the car back to Frances on Bowen. Then I'll start looking for a way to find you again." There was, of course, no answer. In fact, the silence in the car brought Malcolm, not Joey, back to her mind, and she remembered his soft, dry mouth when he'd kissed her.

"Joey, I swear I'll search until I find you."

She should never have let Malcolm kiss her.

Keep on truckin'. Lerner's favourite line. She'd kissed *him* too, without meaning to. As if she'd ever want to kiss Lerner. And here was another saying coined by her generation: *Keep on keeping on.*

She leaned forward over the wheel and searched for the highway turnoff. Instead, her eye lit upon a young woman in a summer dress, walking swiftly along the sidewalk past the shops that lined Lonsdale Avenue. Before Jenny could get a good look at her, the woman ducked into a store. She might have been Moira, but ghosts weren't the only women who wore dresses in summertime. She checked her rear-view. Indeed, several girls sported summer dresses, and the wind from the traffic stirred their skirts as they strolled along the shopfronts.

Jenny braked at the red light at Lonsdale and Twenty-Third. She was in the outside lane, ready to turn onto the highway to the ferry.

She said to herself, "This is a very long light."

Jenny checked her rear-view again. Two green-grape eyes looked back at her from the mirror. Jenny's hands slipped on the wheel, but she pulled herself together. The light changed, and she turned left onto the highway. She kept her foot steady on the gas and her eyes on the road.

She said, "When we get to the island, will you take me back to Lerner's again?"

"What, to your dreary party?" Moira slipped over the seat to sit beside Jenny, in Joey's old spot. "All the gin in the world couldn't make me. Move over."

"What?"

"Move your chassis, sister."

Without willing it, and unsure even as it happened how it happened, Jenny found herself in the passenger seat. Moira took the wheel.

CHAPTER 18

Malcolm willed the bus to move more quickly, so that he had some kind of loser's chance to catch up with Jenny in her cousin's Galaxie. But it was one of those early summer afternoons when everyone was out in cars, and the cars were so jam-packed with dogs and back-seat drivers that they slowed, sped up, and forgot to signal to change lanes. A blonde girl in a construction helmet waved an orange flag to stop the bus as they passed. Malcolm huffed with impatience and sat back in his seat at the front of the bus. In the mirror he caught the bus driver's glare from under his sharp blue cap. This was the broad-backed kind of bus driver, the sort whose blue shirt pulled under his armpits, not the skinny kind that always reeked of cigarettes. The skinny kind drove faster, as a rule.

Malcolm leaned his chin on the back of the seat in front of him and thought about Jenny, about that million-dollar moment when her hand was in his pocket while she kissed him. Or he kissed her. It didn't matter, so long as he caught up with her and told her how he felt, like some kind of hero in a Movie of the Week. Maybe it was better that the bus was moving slowly, because it gave him time to transform into a guy who could say that kind of thing to a beautiful young woman. A hero sort of guy.

The bus driver tooted his horn. There was something about this bus driver that made Malcolm think it might be possible to change the direction of his life. Maybe it was the driver's cap with its sharp blue edge at the brim; it indicated that underneath might reign an organized mind. For the first time since he was a little boy, Malcolm was attracted to the idea of wearing a uniform, which, according to cultural lore, all the girls loved. He explored the idea of giving himself up to an arm of the Canadian military, to be told what to do by perfect strangers—his superiors, people of proven worth within their chosen spheres, and without any familial agenda concerning Malcolm. Of course, the war in Vietnam had lately caused some girls to hate soldiers, no matter how handsome they looked in their caps, and that was also worth considering.

The driver jerked the bus to an unmarked stop. Malcolm peered out the dash window and saw that someone had run out into the road. The bus driver leaned on the horn while a pair of splayed hands, just visible above the wipers, slapped at the bus's windshield.

The bus driver swore and jerked a black shoe onto the brake and then the gas. There was a protesting hiss from the passengers behind Malcolm. The hands at the front window pulled the wipers away from the windshield, and on the other side of the glass, Malcolm made out a crown of yellow hair.

He stood and leaned over the driver's shoulder. Adrian was standing directly in front of the bus. Had he simply walked onto the highway in the hope of stopping it? Malcolm shook his head in disbelief.

The driver pointed with a thick thumb. He shouted through the windshield, "See the sign up ahead on the road? *No Hitchhiking.*" When Adrian didn't move, the driver swung open the door and bellowed through it, "Get out of the way, stupid. You can't get on."

Malcolm saw Adrian's face light up, as if he thought he could get on, was in fact entitled to get on. He loped around to the open door and smacked his sandaled foot down on the step.

"Get the hell off." The bus driver closed the door around Adrian's leg.

"You've stopped already," Adrian said reasonably through the gap, as if this were the normal way to catch a bus on the highway so long as a guy had the *cojones* for it. The traffic growled around them, and the bus driver let the brakes go with a squeal. The bus inched forward so that Adrian had to hop to stay upright.

"Are you nuts?" one of the passengers called out, although it was unclear whether he meant the bus driver or Adrian.

Malcolm stood and grabbed the rail over his head for balance. "Be careful, can't you?"

The bus driver jerked the bus forward another foot, and Adrian's fingers turned white against the folded bus doors.

This was getting serious. Malcolm might have raised his hand against the driver if only he weren't so broad and his hat not so crisp and official. "Cut it out, driver. Anyway, he's looking for me."

The bus driver shoved his shoe back on the brake and looked up at Malcolm. "Oh, well, that's all right then. You get the hell off my bus, too."

Malcolm slung himself over onto the top step of the bus and stared down through the gap at Adrian. "Why are you here? I thought you were on Bowen. I thought you had charge of the kids."

"You think a lot, don't you, Malcolm?" Adrian pulled backwards on the doors, as if they were a puzzle to open and you just had to know the trick.

Malcolm felt the bus driver's hand on his shoulder. The door slammed open, sending Adrian backwards into the dust at the side of the highway. Malcolm was impelled by a push between his shoulder blades that sent him down the steps and out the door. A hot, stinking wind blew away from the bus as it pulled back onto the highway towards the ferry terminal.

Furious, Malcolm stood over Adrian. "How did you know I'd be on this bus?"

"Either I'm magic or you're lucky." Adrian rose to his feet, banging at the dust on his cut-offs. He shrugged. "I've been in town. Had some things to do."

"But you're supposed to be looking after the kids. What things?"

Adrian dug his left hand into his pocket and rustled something there. "Just a little Sunshine."

Sunshine. Otherwise known as LSD. Malcolm rolled his eyes up to the hot blue sky.

Adrian said, "The kids are fine. Everyone worries too much about kids anyway. The little bastards always survive, it's how the species got this far. Listen, stick out your thumb for a ride and you can get back to our campers quick as lightning."

"You're stoned, and I'm not white. Nobody's going to stop for us." Malcolm stuck out his thumb. A car whizzed by, and another.

"Watch me." Adrian stuck his right thumb out too far into the road, where anyone not paying attention could take the whole hand off and drive on without knowing, at least until they found the stain at some later time. Adrian slid his left hand into his pocket. "You know, the thing about me is that you can't even tell. Nobody can tell. Look at me right now. Can you tell?"

"Of course I can tell. It's LSD." But Malcolm couldn't. Adrian looked like he always looked, relaxed and distracted, even with his thumb out dangerously far, not fifty feet from a *No Hitchhiking* sign. A car angled out onto the verge at the side of the highway, but Malcolm didn't like the look of the driver, so he waved it on.

Adrian did not appear to have noticed. "I don't go crazy like some people who take this stuff. I don't throw myself out of windows ..."

"You can't look after kids in your condition."

"Yes, I can. In fact, I like them best like this, and they like me. The thing is — and this is the key — you take the stuff but be yourself. Only better."

"*I* don't like you when you're ... what the hell?" Malcolm spun to watch a green Galaxie whip past them. Adrian raised his thumb again, but the car was already taking the next turn past the *No Hitchhiking* sign. "That was Jenny."

"Wasn't." Adrian took an orange tab stuck to a bit of shiny paper out of his pocket and held it up to Malcolm. "This stuff's clever. You don't often find tasty ones, but these guys know what they're doing. They dip them — "

"That was Frances's Galaxie. Didn't you see the scratch on the bumper? And it was green."

"Green and a Galaxie is a logical fallacy, and you don't want to fall into logical fallacies. For example, aspirins are white and underpants are white. That doesn't mean aspirins are underpants. Let me show you how to think cogently, Malcolm: *that* wasn't Jenny, because Jenny would have stopped for us." Adrian raised his eyebrows.

Malcolm was tired of Adrian being right all the time. Even when he was high, he was right. "Okay, listen. The ferry terminal's that way. I'm going to walk it."

"Walk it! You boring sod. If you weren't Chinese, you'd be underpants white."

"Shut up." Malcolm couldn't call Adrian a racist, because he wasn't. All he could do was walk away.

Adrian seized Malcolm by the collar and turned him round. "Malcolm, seriously. Only you could go on a girl hunt, get kicked off a bus, stand in rushing traffic, and make it look boring. So if I give you one, will you take it?"

"One what?" He tried to pull his shirt loose, but Malcolm hadn't out-muscled Adrian since they were four.

"Sunshine." Adrian held the tablet up on its little bit of paper while traffic roared and Malcolm struggled. Letting go of his shirt, Adrian snatched Malcolm's hand and folded the tab into it. He licked the orange residue from his own palm.

Malcolm stared down at the tiny disk. It was a dull, unnatural orange, not so bright as the construction girl's flag. Like orange-flavoured candy stuck on paper.

Adrian closed Malcolm's fingers around it.

"I don't want it."

"You can always get what you don't want," Adrian sang. "But when you do, don't let people see what's going on in your head. Be cool."

"I'm always cool."

"You're always *quiet*."

"Says you." But of course Adrian was correct. Adrian was the cool one, always had been since they were little boys, Malcolm in a bow tie, at their mothers' bridge teas.

"Never tell anybody anything." Adrian took another from his pocket and flicked at the orange tab with his thumb.

Malcolm held his own thumb up to his nose. It smelled of orange, or the way the modern world thought orange smelled, anyway. Like Tang or orange Jell-O. Maybe he was imagining the smell, though. He touched the tip of his tongue to the pill and tasted bitterness. He muttered, "I'd never throw myself out of windows thinking I can fly. I'd never run out into the traffic. Hey!"

Adrian ran out into the traffic. A second green Galaxie bowled by him at top speed. It roared away along the highway towards the ferry terminal.

Adrian stood in the middle of the road in his dusty shorts, head back and arms extended like John the Baptist in cut-off shorts, while the draft from passing traffic whipped up his yellow shirt at the back. A third green Galaxie headed straight for him. Malcolm felt his blood rise as he realized that the Galaxie couldn't slow down in time. Couldn't, in fact, miss Adrian.

But it did. The car veered and swiped at the side of Adrian's shorts. Malcolm thought the driver, whom he couldn't see, was sure to stop and swear at them, but the car tore away from them down the highway without stopping.

Adrian dodged back through traffic, putting his middle finger up at a red Strato-Chief that growled past. "Holy crap, did you see that?"

"Are you trying to kill yourself?"

The words hung for a moment in the shining white air of the afternoon.

Adrian closed his eyes and laughed. "Not right this moment, brother." He slipped his hand back into his pocket. "*That* was Jenny's car."

"Then why didn't Jenny stop?"

Adrian opened his eyes and looked straight at Malcolm. "What are you talking about? It was the *car*. Frances's Galaxie. But Jenny wasn't driving it."

"Who was?" Malcolm demanded.

Adrian shrugged.

That was twice in one day Malcolm had felt like punching somebody. "I don't need you. I'll find her myself."

Malcolm set off at a brisk stride along the road towards the ferry terminal, hoping there would be another bus stop along the way. If not, he'd walk on. Adrian could follow or not. If he did, Adrian could eat his dust.

"Some other girl was driving," Adrian called after him. Malcolm looked over his shoulder, tripped on a rock, and almost fell beneath the wheels of a honking semi. He turned.

"*What* other girl?" Malcolm shouted. Adrian held up his expressive middle finger again.

Malcolm swore, turned his back on Adrian, and ran. It was that kind of day. He hadn't run this much since high school. With every step he took towards Jenny, he was more certain he was travelling in the right direction.

Just as Adrian caught up with him, another bus approached from behind, and even though there was no bus stop here, this bus actually stopped without being flagged down. The door huffed open and the young bus driver, blond hair shining under his peaked driver's cap, winked at him. Malcolm slipped Adrian's LSD into one pocket of his jeans and fished in the other for a quarter. Adrian could find his own fare. Of course, Adrian did.

"Thanks for stopping for us." Malcolm leaned forward to speak to the driver from his spot up front while Adrian roamed the back rows of the bus. "We'd have had a long walk if you hadn't."

"Just let me drive, man," the driver said. His blond hair was longer than you'd expect for a bus driver.

"The bus wasn't supposed to pick you up," the old woman sitting next to Malcolm said. "Vehicles ought not to stop on the Upper Levels highway, unless it's for a deer. You wouldn't want to hit a deer, would you?"

"I would if I wanted a crapload of venison," the driver said.

The old woman shook her head. "He's unexpectedly vulgar, isn't he?"

"How long to the ferry terminal?" Malcolm asked.

"Most days, it takes as long as it takes." The bus driver hunched his shoulders.

"And, rude, ruder, rudest!" The old woman to Malcolm's right leaned across the aisle and patted Malcolm's seat as if it were part of him, like his thigh. "He's very young for a bus driver, though. Most young people are so impolite, aren't they? I know *I* was." Her knuckles bulged over the chrome seat rail in front of her as the bus driver swerved for no reason that Malcolm could see.

Malcolm muttered, "He's young and he's mean, but I don't care as long as he drives like stink."

The bus juddered.

"Are we slowing down?" Malcolm asked the old woman.

"I don't think so, dear." She leaned forward. "Say, driver. How do you get to be a bus driver anyway? I only ask because I have a grandson."

The bus driver snorted. "I just find myself here in this seat every day, opening and closing the doors."

Malcolm wondered, if he decided once and for all not to be a doctor, whether he might end up strapped into a seat like this guy, opening and closing doors — or the geometrical career equivalent of opening and closing doors. He asked, "But if you don't want to drive buses anymore, can't you just walk away?"

"Can't walk away." Usually you could look up and meet the driver's eye in the mirror, but this guy had it tilted so that all you saw was his blue cotton collar. Open. No tie. When he answered, Malcolm couldn't tell whether it was to the old woman or Malcolm himself.

The bus driver said, "I've got responsibilities and a girl I need to take care of. Now shut up so I can get you where you want to go."

"Is your girlfriend waiting for you?" the old woman asked. "Does she love you heart and soul? That's always nice, isn't it?"

"She's a loyal girl," the bus driver said. "She can be counted on."

"I meant you, dear." She nodded at Malcolm. "Is *your* love properly requited?"

"Well …" Malcolm hesitated. "I guess I'm working on that."

"You *guess?*" The bus driver snorted. "Doesn't sound like the world's romance to me."

She leaned closer. "Are you her hero? That's how you know."

Malcolm edged towards the window. "I don't know if she's the type to have one of those."

"All girls have a hero," the bus driver said. "I'd bet money that if you're not it, there is some other fellow — maybe somebody who came before you, somebody she loved all her life — that even a smart guy like you would never in a million years be able to replace. That's her hero."

"I can't imagine that you're interested in my love life, driver." This driver reminded Malcolm of Adrian, both of them gifted at making him feel like a dud.

The old woman held onto the seat rail with both hands. She gave a long sigh that smelled of camphor and onions. "We're just worried about you. It's natural to worry about sad young men like yourself. I knew a woman with a grandson your age, handsome and funny as he could be. One afternoon he sat on his bed cross-legged and took a lot of *something*, with a note in his pocket to say he had no friends. Doctors couldn't save him."

Malcolm asked, "Took a lot of what? Pills? Were they orange ones?"

"He had no friends at all. But the funeral was full of young people, and they were all crying."

"All the youth do drugs," the bus driver said. The driver wasn't much older than Malcolm, judging by his hands and the way his clean short fingernails looked new—almost unused. And he wore blue jeans and Adidas, unlike the previous driver. But he sounded like an old fellow when he asked, "I bet *you* do drugs, don't you, kid?"

Malcolm ducked his head to see the driver's face, but he couldn't find the angle. "I'm possibly the only person my age not to do them," he said. He sounded like he needed his childhood bow tie back around his neck. "I mean, I don't like to be out of control, you know?"

"*Good* for you," the old woman said. She slapped the rail in front of her seat.

Malcolm felt in his shorts pocket for the orange tablet Adrian had given him. Then he felt in his other pocket. He skewed around to see whether it might have fallen out onto the bus seat or the floor.

"How old *are* you, driver?" the woman asked. "I ask because I have a grandson who'd like to drive ..."

"I'm twenty-two," the driver answered. "This is the stop for ferry foot passengers. And my free advice to you, guy, is to find yourself another girl. A girl who's one-hundred-percent all yours, without heavy baggage from an earlier relationship. Take it from one who knows." He slammed at the lever and the door slapped open. "Remember, you've got to have someone who cares when you die."

"*I'd* care," the old lady said. "I certainly care whether you die while you're driving this bus."

Malcolm jumped down the two steps and onto the road. Adrian loped past him and across to the ticket booth. Malcolm stood in front of the bus door, feeling around in his pockets for the little paper with LSD stuck to it. He couldn't find it, but surely he'd remember if he'd taken Adrian's orange-flavoured Sunshine.

He glanced at the ferryboat, turned, and banged on the bus door. The door squeaked open, the flaps slipping across the palms of his hands. Hot exhaust blew into his nose.

"Do you want Park Royal Shopping Centre?" the driver asked him.

"I want to take another look around my seat. I think I lost something." Malcolm peered up at the first seat on the left, to ask the old woman to help him search for the missing orange disc. But she wasn't there. In her place, a little girl was dangling both arms over the bar at the front of the seat. Her nose was running. She wiped it on her wrist and rolled her eyes at him.

The driver was a stranger as well. He had to be sixty years old, at the least. "Where are you going, son?"

Malcolm backed down the steps. He could make the ferry sailing, easy. He felt in his pocket and pulled out a couple of bucks, exactly enough for the fare. He paid his fare at the ticket booth and dashed along the chicken-wire fence to the ferry ramp. He might have inadvertently taken LSD, or not; but he was certain that having the right number of dollar bills in his hand exactly when he needed them meant that the world was set up so that Jenny would love him. This feeling, so universal that there were songs of love on everyone's lips at every moment of the day all around the world, had to be genetically engineered into the human biochemical setup to be reciprocal. Love was in fact more likely than not to be returned, or else it would not have survived with the species. It was scientifically, maybe even mathematically, inevitable. Equations must balance, of course they did, the way doors opened and shut. Ergo, if he felt this way, then in some combination of the integers of her soul, Jenny might feel this way too. He could well win this subtle and unresponsive girl. He banished from his head the hundreds of sad love songs that said he wouldn't.

"Anyway," Malcolm said aloud, his feet pounding across the ferry ramp, "you've got to have somebody who cares if you die."

CHAPTER 19

Unnoticed by humans, birds, and dogs leashed or unleashed, Joey strolled along the beach between the ferry berth and the marina. He took off his bus driver's cap, held it by the sharp blue brim, and studied it from all sides. In life, he'd eschewed all headgear, and it was a revelation how much authority a bit of stiffened navy fabric gave a guy.

He murmured, "Malcolm, you are such an easy mark." Joey would never be more than knee-jerk jealous of a loser like that. Holding the cap between thumb and forefinger, he brought it back to his chest and flung it spinning out to sea. It flew like a bird, like a plane, like a rocket for Mars.

You could do lots of things when you were dead. Walk on water was one of them. He did so now, pacing the shallows towards the deep waters of Howe Sound. He thought he'd probably be able to fly as well, to soar blue-jeaned against the blue sky. One of these days he'd do it. Yes, one of these empty, lukewarm days he'd take off up where the blue air thins to black. Up, up, and away, and all alone.

But *why* was he so damned alone all the time? This whole death business was a screw-up. Joey was never meant to be alone. Even when he died, Jenny had been with him.

"You said you'd always be there for me, Jenny," he called. There was no answer. There wasn't even an echo. His voice flew off across the water on the light offshore wind.

And another thing — why was he the only dead person on this beach? Everybody died. There ought to be legions of heart attack cases cluttering up the sky, moaning and bitching like old people did, about who-knew-what. He couldn't care less about dead old people. What young person cared about them, if they were honest enough to admit it? Seriously, no lie. The old ones didn't care about the young ones either.

"At least," he called out, "mine was a very happy childhood."

No answer. He gazed into the shining sky and thought about the dance he'd been at. What a bore! Maybe ghosts were all like those foxtrotting fools and that silly, pretty girl who had it in for Jenny. He'd given that his best shot. What more could he do?

He had a new thought. A couple of months before, when he'd died, flying had been his first and most obvious wish, but he'd decided that was for eager little kids who wanted to be superheroes or pilots. How might he soar and keep his cool?

Maybe he'd remove the effort from the process and drift up into the sky, where he'd become blue-jean bluer and bluer as the day wore on. Rise higher and higher. He chuckled. Lord knew that was what he'd wanted all his life, to get higher and higher. Since he'd died, he didn't want the stuff—didn't want the drinks or the drugs. That crap was for the living, and he didn't begrudge them their orange-coloured tongues or the moment they fell over into … into what? Joey couldn't remember now. Perhaps he didn't care to.

James Dean died young. Joey wondered whether James Dean had cared about his family or worried that they missed him. Whether he did or didn't, they'd learned to live without him by now, and so would Joey's family and friends. Save one.

"God, I miss you, Jenny," he said aloud. He turned in a quiet arc on the surface of the water, his arms out.

If only she were here. If only she would look him in the eye like she used to and talk with him the way they used to do, with no one in between them. He'd show her that dying was not an end. It was a *process*. He grimaced, remembering how he used to try to share with her the process of finding the high. But maybe this time she'd listen, now that things were serious.

He balanced one Adidas-shod foot on a wave and let it carry him further out into the water.

Jenny would listen and do what he said, because if there was one thing she knew, it was that he'd never told a lie in his life.

"I'm honest, and also I died so young," he said to the sky. It gleamed right back at him, as if it were a perfect blue bubble that had never heard of smog or three-stage rockets to the moon. Even the sky lied. Everyone lied except him.

"All I need is the air …" Joey hummed.

But he didn't. He didn't need anything. No air, no drink, no food. Just Jenny. She was the only habit, good or bad, that he hadn't left behind.

"I'm a better person already," he called out, though he wasn't sure to whom. Certainly, no one answered. He felt cold, and unstable on his feet considering he was only twenty-two.

On his right hand, the ferry sounded its blasted horn and pulled out. He stumbled in its wake and nearly fell down into the water.

Loneliness took hold of his heart and steadied him like hands from behind.

He was not a person who should be alone. Jenny was his girl, and although he wasn't exactly angry that she had abandoned him now, just when he needed her most, the fact was hardly pleasing. Death was a hard enough pill to swallow without knowing he'd lost his best girl—and maybe to an awkward, overthinking science student at that. He summoned his own cool, and it came to heel like a good dog, like a guardian angel.

Keep your head up, Malcolm.

He looked down at his empty hands and wished that he had his peaked hat back again—to toss it, with cool, back into the ring.

Chapter 20

One minute Jenny was Moira's passenger in the Galaxie on the highway to the ferry; the next, Moira reached across, pushed open Jenny's door, and shoved her out of the car. Jenny fell and rolled, not onto tarmac or the rocky ridge of the road, but onto the gritty floor of a busy, music-filled hall. This was not a good spot to sit on her backside and consider her surroundings, for there were dancers moving all around her, and the song was so jazzy that she couldn't hope they'd miss her with their leather brogues and Cuban heels. She scrambled to her feet and moved among the dancers, looking for Joey, because who else would she know here apart from Moira? But once she'd circled the room twice, she admitted to herself that just because she had crossed from the land of the living, it didn't mean she'd find Joey here. This was not Joey's kind of party. Not at all.

Nor was it hers. She disliked the packed space with its brassy, corny band, people pushing her, and the smell of everybody's underarms. Out of the circling crowd of dancers, three couples bumped into her, one after another. She blinked to clear her vision and looked up into the shiny black eyes of a slick-haired man in a white suit under a mirror ball. He was almost kissing his microphone. He met her gaze and nodded as if he'd seen her here before.

"*I bought my love a Deusenberg, the longest ever sold,*" the bandleader sang. "*To take my Dora home from sharing 'round her heart of gold.*"

The only good thing about the place was that Moira wasn't here. Or she wasn't here yet. Was the ghost still driving the Galaxie? Jenny could only hope to high heaven that she'd pull off the road and leave the Upper Levels traffic unharmed.

Hands seized Jenny's shoulders and turned her around. A redheaded man slipped his arm about her and pulled her into the centre of the floor to do an old ballroom dance called the foxtrot, one they still taught you in high school. She wasn't much of a one for ballroom dancing—Joey had ranked it with bowling for lack of cool—but it was not a bad way to check out the dance hall for an exit. And it gave her somebody to hide behind if Moira turned up, as she was bound to do soon.

"Stop leading," the redheaded man said. "You're not the best dancer, kiddo. Let's climb outside and have a drink."

Outside. Away from here. "All right," Jenny said. "I'll follow you. Where's the door?"

Before he could answer, a woman in nurse's whites danced up to them, took the redhead by the hand, and fox-trotted him away.

"Cause all the money in the world won't stop a jealous man," the bandleader sang. *"Nor all the sweetness in the world can make him understand."* Behind him, the saxophone player buzzed a lick between verses.

This was Moira's kind of place, all right, and it was easy to imagine her pushing through the crowd, looking for her Philip. When she didn't find him, she'd take Jenny by the wrist. And then what? Do the arithmetic, Jenny told herself. Moira had been dead for forty years. Had she spent much of her time here? Jenny had no wish to do the same. She had her own fellow to look for, and Joey had his own kind of party. That's where she would find him. Back at Lerner's party house. The house that had vanished. The house that had been, in the real world, torn down. But she'd seen it whole again, hadn't she, the last time she'd visited? And if, in this world, the house returned like the memory it was, then might she not find Joey and the boys gathered in Lerner's velvet dark living room, listening to *Speed King*? If this were indeed the ghost world, then, like Orpheus, she had arrived where a living being had no right to be. How she hoped that the ancient story was true, and not just a lie so pretty that it had never over thousands of years been forgotten. Like Orpheus, she'd quest for her dead true love. She knew how the age-old story ended, but this was now, and she was new.

"*Hey Dora, Dora Heart, hi-dee hi-dee hi,*" the bandleader sang. "*Dora walked away along the highway in the sky.*"

Walk away. Jenny shoved through the dancers towards the wall. She still couldn't see a door, but a row of windows stood open to the night air. In front of the windows, a line of older women sat chatting. She excused herself, slipped between two of them, and hauled herself up onto the windowsill. She swung her legs over the sill and knocked her ankle bones. A last look back showed no sign of Moira in the crowd. She wanted to ask these older women please not to tell Moira where she'd gone, but their sharp eyes and folded mouths made them look the sort of folks who wouldn't do her any favours.

She lowered herself from the window to the ground, a distance of only five feet or so. An easy drop.

She found herself standing in complete darkness, aware of rough rocks underfoot and the sound of quiet water.

The water was on her left. The dance hall was behind her, and the pit-deep darkness on her right didn't encourage exploration. Jenny held out both arms for balance and walked forward, each step too hurried for safety on the rocky surface. If she kept on, she must eventually find her way to somewhere different. If she were lucky, she would find the place Joey was, at Lerner's mystic party house. Furthermore, in a place like this where rules were off, finding Joey might not be entirely a question of luck. She'd made it into the ghost world, and Joey might very well sense she was here, that she'd made it across whatever passed for a River Styx in this time and place. If he knew, he'd come find her. Of that she was perfectly certain.

Strong hands took Jenny by the shoulders and stopped her dead. She smelled alcohol — subtle and unflavoured, but unmistakable.

She'd smelled it on Joey often enough. She pulled free, turned, and pushed Moira away from her.

"Don't push me," Moira said.

"Don't grab me," Jenny said. "And stop chasing me everywhere. It's not dignified, Moira. Get some self-respect."

"All I'm trying to do is get you to help me find Philip. I don't know why you can't understand."

"Here's what I don't get: why me? I don't even know what your guy looks like. And I don't know how long I'll be able to stay in this place, so stop wasting my time."

Jenny turned her back on Moira and felt her way along a little farther down the beach. Moira hurried up beside her and walked between Jenny and the sound of the water.

Moira said, "It doesn't matter that you don't know what Philip looks like. What matters is that you search for him with me. That for the first time in yonks I have a friend, an ally in love and war. I've been searching alone for longer than I can tell you, and it's always the same. Dancing, searching, the same old songs, the same old mirror ball, and I never find him."

Jenny felt a pang of sympathy. "Look. What if you let him find you instead?"

"Thanks so much indeed for the agony-aunt advice, sister," Moira said. "Sure. You think I haven't tried it? I go to the ship where he works and I ..." Moira trailed off.

"Go on, damn it. You what?"

"I try to get his attention. And no matter how often I try, he doesn't find me. He doesn't see no matter what I do. But maybe if there were two of us, we'd be somehow different. Not just dance, search, dance, climb and jump ..."

Jenny interrupted. "What do you mean, climb and jump?"

"It doesn't matter."

"It sounds like it matters. I think you need to stop whatever that is."

Moira said, "I'll stop it if you help me."

Jenny threw both arms wide. "I helped you. I went to your sweaty, croony foxtrot dance, and I didn't find your Philip. Now will you please go look for your boyfriend and let me try to find mine?"

Moira didn't answer, and Jenny walked on, apparently alone. Pebbles rattled underneath her flip-flops until footsteps caught up to her again.

A subdued Moira asked out of the darkness behind her, "Did you really not see anybody in the dance hall? Tell me the truth."

"Not your Philip. Not my Joey. Not even you."

"I can't see you well enough to tell whether you're lying."

"I'm not lying."

"I want to know for sure. Step into the water where I can see you." Moira pulled Jenny into the shallows.

Jenny meant to say that Moira was being ridiculous, that it was as dark at sea as on land at night; but when the two moved left, sure enough, a grey light poured across the water. She saw Moira clearly now, nearly up to her dress hem in the water.

The ghost took Jenny by the elbows and looked closely into her eyes. "I knew it. Something's different about you since yesterday. What happened?"

Jenny felt herself colour. "Nothing."

"Something. You kissed somebody. Or somebody kissed you." Moira's grip tightened. "Did you kiss my Philip?"

"Of course I didn't. I never met him in my life."

"Some girls will kiss a stranger." Moira's green gaze met hers again. "Swear you didn't?"

"Yes."

"Then was it your true love you kissed?"

"No, it wasn't. In fact, I don't know how I happened to kiss him."

"Oh, an accidental kiss? Like a handkerchief dropped on the sidewalk, and some fellow just picks it up? That kind of kiss?"

"Listen ..." Jenny left the word there as a marker. She pulled away from Moira and splashed out of the water, back into darkness, to continue her progress along the rocky shoreline, with Moira almost certainly at her heels. And it had to happen: Jenny tripped, stumbled, and fell. Moira wrapped her fingers through Jenny's hair and pulled hard.

Jenny cried out and pushed herself up onto her knees, the small rocks sharp against her skin.

Moira let go. "Don't be such a baby. I'm just trying to show you what it feels like when your best friend hurts *you.*"

Jenny's stomach felt like a small hard fist. "Moira, my best friend is dead. Joey's *dead*, and so are ..."

"*Don't* say another word."

Jenny took a step away, but Moira caught her, and not just by her arm or even her hair. This time it felt as if Moira poured right over Jenny like a sucking wave and pulled her down the beach into the water.

Jenny had sense enough to take a breath. At least she had the good sense to take that last deep breath. Moira pulled Jenny along through the shallows over the barnacle rocks, down into the dark water, and out to sea. They held on tight to each other, like mermaid sisters.

THE ARTISTS

AKEM
Cover artist, Collector
Akem is a writer, an illustrator, and an artist in animation. She illustrated *Brown Sugar Babe*, a picture book about the beauty of dark skin, in 2020. Her fantasy stories can be found in *Augur Magazine* and *Polar Borealis*. Akem's story 'Shotguns and Jinn' appears in *Pulp Literature* Issue 25, and her cover art graces issues 16 (*Seabus*), 18 (*Windseeker*), and 23 (*Greetings*). A compilation of her personal and published artwork can be found at akemiart.ca.

ALLISON BANNISTER
Line artist and author, 'The Play's the Thing'
Allison Bannister is a cartoonist and comics scholar with an MFA in Cartoon Studies and a PhD in Communication and Rhetoric. She writes and draws comics about ghosts, magic, and dinosaurs, tending toward stories about getting lost and finding a new way home. She teaches writing and visual storytelling. 'The Play's the Thing' is loosely based on her childhood amateur Shakespeare troupe and was originally published in the Shakespeare tribute anthology *My Kingdom for a Panel*. Allison's graphic short 'Ghost Room' appears in *Pulp Literature* Issue 25, Winter 2020. You can find more of her work at basictelepathy.com.

Tom O'Brien
Colourist, 'The Play's the Thing'

Tom O'Brien is a cartoonist and illustrator. His work ranges from fantasy to non-fiction, and he is currently working on a long-form comic about the use and care of kitchen knives. His work can be found at tomobriencomics.com, and in anthologies, including *Who is the Silhouette?*, *Ever Afterward*, and *My Kingdom for a Panel*. Outside of comics, he works part-time at a kitchen-supply store and enjoys audiobooks, video games, and RPGs.

Mel Anastasiou
In-house illustrator

Mel Anastasiou loves drawing for *Pulp Literature* because she loves the stories she illustrates. She draws in black and white, working from imagination and inspired by details from Renaissance compositions. You can find illustrations, writing tips, and news about her books and novellas at melanastasiou.wordpress.com, and see more of her artwork on Facebook at Bird and Branch Artwork.

HALL OF FAME

*These are the heroes — the Patrons and Pulp Literati whose monthly support
helped bring you this issue. Please lift your glasses and give them a rousing cheer!*

The Brewers
Robin McGillveray

The Landlords
Isabel Cushey
Dana Tye Rally

The Innkeepers
Ada Maria Soto
Margot Landels
Ev Bishop
Shannon Saunders
Roger & Anne Anastasiou
Kevin Harris
Gillian Gardiner
Megan Shaw
Susan Jackson
Richard Ohnemus
Nicole Clark

The Bartenders
Alana Krider
Richard Gropp
Ron Graves
Kristen Mah
Victoria McAuley
Dave Wayne
Scott F Gray

Michelle Balfour
Abigail Bruce
Vernice Dietra Malik
Katriona Greenmoor
KT Wagner
Deepthi Atukorala
Margot Spronk
Margaret Elliott
Peter Halasz
Bjarne Hansen
Leny Wagner
Kain Stewart
Chris Olee
kc dyer
Kimberley Aslett
Jan Fagan
Ken Oakes
Brighton Hugg
Alexa Benzaid-
Williams
Bryan Moose
Maureen Cooke
Katja Rammer
Kelly Fahy
Mark Catalfano
Norm Rosolen
K Anastasiou
Mike Sylvester

Wichael Tellez
Katherine Derbyshire
Kerri Chamberlin
Rapscallion

The Regulars
CC Humphreys
Marta Salek
Rina Piccolo
Emily Lonie
Jenny Blackford
Jain Cairns
Akemi Art
BC
Meredith Frazier
Catherine Levinson
Vera
Charity Tahmaseb
Alexander Langer
Marilyn Holt
Risa Wolf
David Perlmutter
Adrienne Wood
Jo Heckman
Cris Martinez

*If you would like to join the ranks of these worthies, you can become a patron
on Patreon at patreon.com/pulplit or join the Pulp Literati through our website
at pulpliterature.com/join-pulp-literati/.*

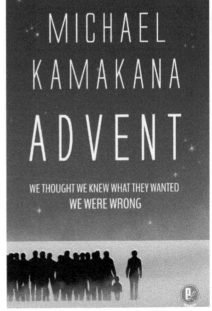

EVENT Magazine's 35th Annual

NON-FICTION CONTEST

INCREASED CASH PRIZES

DEADLINE:
OCTOBER 15

$1,500 • $1,000 • $500

Non-Fiction Contest winners feature in every volume since 1989 and have received recognition from the **Canadian Magazine Awards, National Magazine Awards and Best Canadian Essays.** All entries considered for publication. Entry fee of $34.95 includes a one-year subscription. We encourage writers from diverse backgrounds and experience levels to submit their work.

EVENTMAGAZINE.CA

BRITISH COLUMBIA
ARTS COUNCIL
An agency of the Province of British Columbia

Canada Council   Conseil des arts
for the Arts   du Canada

DOUGLAS
DOUGLAS COLLEGE
douglascollege.ca

THE LABOURS OF MRS STELLA RYMAN
FURTHER FAIRMOUNT MANOR MYSTERIES

When the machineries of institution fail to protect Fairmount Manor, octogenarian amateur sleuth Mrs Stella Ryman rolls up her fleece jacket sleeves to ferret out a thief, investigate a gun-toting resident, set right a mishandled investigation of a man's death, pursue spectres and footpads walking at midnight, and discover Thelma Hu's long-lost fortune.

BOOK II OF THE FAIRMOUNT MANOR MYSTERIES
BY MEL ANASTASIOU, AVAILABLE NOW
FROM PULP LITERATURE PRESS

PULPLITERATURE.COM/STELLA-RYMAN
ISBN (PRINT): 978-1-988865-11-9
ISBN (EBOOK): 978-1-988865-12-6

MARKETPLACE

*B*OOKS

Advent *by Michael Kamakana* • We thought we knew what the aliens wanted. Think again. • pulpliterature.com/advent

Allaigna's Song: Chorale *by JM Landels* • The long-awaited conclusion to the bestselling *Allaigna's Song* trilogy. • pulpliterature.com/allaignas-song

The Extra: A Monument Studios Mystery *by Mel Anastasiou* • Extra Frankie Ray gets her big break on the Silver Screen—until Murder steals the scene. • pulpliterature.com/the-extra

The Labours of Mrs Stella Ryman: Further Fairmount Mysteries *by Mel Anastasiou* • Trapped in a down-at-the-heels care home. You'd be cranky too. • pulpliterature.com/stella-ryman-and-the-fairmount-manor-mysteries

What the Wind Brings *by Matthew Hughes* • Winner of the 2020 Endeavour Award • pulpliterature.com/product-category/novels/matthew-hughes

The Writer's Boon Companion *by Mel Anastasiou* • Thirty Days Towards an Extraordinary Volume • pulpliterature.com/subscribe/the-bookstore

Bookstores

Book Warehouse · 632 Broadway W, Vancouver, BC V5Z 1G1 · 604-872-5711 bookwarehouse.ca

Phoenix On Bowen · 992 Dorman Rd, Bowen Island, BC V0N 1G0 · 604-947-2793

Village Books & Coffee House · 130-12031 First Ave, Richmond, BC V7E 3M1 604-272-6601 · villagebooks@shaw.ca

Western Sky Books · 2132-2850 Shaughnessy St, Port Coquitlam, BC V3C 6K5 · 604-461-5602 · store.westernskybooks.com

White Dwarf / Dead Write Books · 3715 10th Ave W, Vancouver, BC V6R 2G5 · 604-228-8223 · whitedwarf@deadwrite.com

Conferences & Events

Word on the Lake · May 2023 · Salmon Arm, BC · wordonthelakewritersfestival.com

When Words Collide · August 2022 Calgary, AB · whenwordscollide.org

Wine Country Writers' Festival · 23-24 Sep 2023 · winecountrywriters-festival.ca

Surrey International Writers' Conference October 2022 · siwc.ca

Magazines

Amazing Stories · Back in print! amazingstories.com

The Digest Enthusiast · Digests past & present plus new genre fiction larquepress.com

EVENT Magazine · Poetry & prose eventmagazine.ca

Geist Ideas + Culture · Made in Canada geist.com

Mystery Magazine · The cutting edge of short mystery fiction www.mysteryweekly.com

Neo-opsis · Canadian magazine of science fiction based in Victoria, BC · neo-opsis.ca

OnSpec · The Canadian magazine of the fantastic · onspecmag.wordpress.com

Polar Borealis · Paying market for new Canadian SF&F writers & artists · polarborealis.ca

Room Magazine · Literature, Art & Feminism since 1975 · roommagazine.com

Printing & Publishing

First Choice Books/Victoria Bindery Book printing & binding · graphic design · eBooks · marketing materials 1-800-957-0561 · firstchoicebooks.ca

Writing Resources

Dreamers Creative Writing · Workshops, residencies, contests & more! · www.dreamerswriting.com

Quit the Day Job · A school for writers from Pulp Literature Press pulpliterature.com/quit-the-day-job

The Writers' Lodge on Bowen Island The Muse retreats for writers · pulpliterature.com/calendar-of-events/retreats/

Room Magazine

2022 Contest Calendar

Creative Non-Fiction

1st Prize: $1000 + publication
2nd Prize: $250 + publication
April 1 - June 15

Poetry

1st Prize: $1000 + publication
2nd Prize: $250 + publication
June 15 - August 31

Short Forms

1st Prize: $500 + publication
(two awarded)
September 1 - November 15

Covert Art

1st Prize: $500 + publication
2nd Prize: $50 + publication
November 15 - January 15, 2023

ROOM

Making Space in Literature, Art & Feminism Since 1975

Entry Fee: $35 (for entrants residing in Canada), $45 (for entrants residing in USA), $55 (for entrants residing anywhere else). Entry includes a one-year subscription to *Room*. Additional entries $7. Visit roommagazine.com/contest

CONTESTS

Pulp Literature runs four annual contests for poetry, flash fiction, and short stories. For contest guidelines, prizes, and entry fees, see pulpliterature.com/contests.

The Raven Short Story Contest
Contest opens: 1 September 2022
Deadline: 15 October 2022
Winner notified: 15 November 2022
Winner published: Issue 38, Spring 2023
Prize: $300

The Bumblebee Flash Fiction Contest
Contest opens: 1 January 2023
Deadline: 15 February 2023
Winner notified: 15 March 2023
Winner published: Issue 39, Summer 2023
Prize: $300

The Magpie Award for Poetry
Contest opens: 1 March 2023
Deadline: 15 April 2023
Winner notified: 15 May 2023
Winner published: Issue 40, Autumn 2023
Prize: $500

The Hummingbird Flash Fiction Prize
Contest opens: 1 May 2023
Deadline: 15 June 2023
Winner notified: 15 July 2022
Winner published: Issue 41, Winter 2024
Prize: $300

ℬECOME A PATRON OF PULP LITERATURE

By supporting *Pulp Literature* on Patreon with $2 or more per month, you will be laying the foundation for a secure future for the magazine, as well as ensuring that you never miss an issue! Your subscription includes four big issues of short stories, novellas, poetry, comics, and novel excerpts, delivered to your door or electronic mailbox each year. **Find us at patreon.com/pulplit**

If you prefer to subscribe through our website, go to pulpliterature.com/subscribe.

Or you can send a cheque with the form below to
Subscriptions, Pulp Literature Press, 21955 16 Ave, Langley BC, V2Z 1K5, Canada

Don't miss an issue!

- ❑ **Send me 2 years (8 issues) at the special rate of $90** (save $30)*
- ❑ **Send me 1 year (4 issues) for $50** (save $10)*
- ❑ **Send me 2 years of digital issues for $30** (save $9.92)
- ❑ **Send me 1 year of digital issues for $17.50** (save $2.47)

Name: _____

Address: _____

City: _____ Prov. / State: _____

Postal code: _____ Country:_____

Email: _____

- ❑ Payment enclosed
- ❑ Bill me
- ❑ New
- ❑ Renewal

Make cheques payable in Canadian funds to Pulp Literature Press. Include email address for digital editions and Paypal billing, or subscribe at www.pulpliterature.com.

*for postage outside Canada add $20 per year in North America or $36 per year overseas.

Ingram Content Group UK Ltd.
Milton Keynes UK
UKHW032028100423
419806UK00019B/566

9 781988 865492